This Road Tonight
A New Pilgrim's Progress

A Novel by Steven Case

the apocryphile press
BERKELEY, CA
www.apocryphile.org

apocryphile press
BERKELEY, CA

Apocryphile Press
1700 Shattuck Ave #81
Berkeley, CA 94709
www.apocryphile.org

Printed in the United States of America
ISBN 9781940671475

This Road Tonight
A New Pilgrim's Progress

A Novel by Steven Case

Dedication

This book is dedicated to the memory of Rev. Carl Pierson. He will always be the Preacher to me.

And to my wife Becky. When the minister announces that the bride and groom are now "one," they are no more "one" than they were a moment before. "One" takes time. "One" happens slowly. My wife and I have become "one." She is all of me and I am all of her—"One."

Acknowledgments

Mark Oestricher, who asked, "Have you ever read *A Pilgrim's Progress*"?

John Mabry, who asked, "Can you give me risky Christian fiction?"

Mr. John Bunyan, who wrote the original.

Lost and Found, who wrote the song "Lions" and "Lift My Eyes," have given me faith and hope beyond understanding. www.speedwood.com

Trader Joe's. I have previously acknowledged the serious amount of their coffee I consumed while writing this and other books. I do so again in the hopes of a freebie. Here's hoping third time's the charm.

All my students...ever...both past and present...you are in here.

And Faith, who became very real to me as I wrote this book.

Introduction

This book is allegory...but we'll get to that shortly.

The original version of *The Pilgrim's Progress* was written by John Bunyan and published in 1678. He went to prison for a short time just for writing it. I'm guessing the worst that will happen now is a few angry emails.

There have been many "revised" editions, graphic novels, re-printings, and one slightly disturbing version, written in the 50's, called *A Young Pilgrim's Progress*, in which the main characters are portrayed as children lost and alone in a big scary world where horrible things happen to them.

It has been translated into more than 200 languages and has never been out of print. The story is timeless because what-ever your age, whatever your generation, wherever you are in you own life-journey...you can find yourself in these pages. Somewhere. What's odd is I don't see myself in the story now as I did when I began the new version. My place in my own journey has changed so much that the way I view the story has changed as well. The book can be read and re-read. It can be read by a dozen people in a book club, and none of them will see themselves in the same place.

Which brings us to allegory...

Allegory is a literary device. The characters and the events they go through are meant to have a larger meaning. None of it is to be taken literally. Sometimes the purpose of allegory is to make complicated ideas easily understood.

Sometimes we use allegory to make hard truths more digestible.

When you read in this story that the City of Moraltown is built on the edge of a cliff and is held up by rotting timbers, it's pretty easy to see the allegory there. Other allegories may not be so easy. Some may come back to you down the road on some idle Tuesday when something you read and discarded suddenly has meaning.

You are in these pages. We all are.

Find yourself.

Chapter 1

His name was Christian.

He stood outside, in front of the house where he grew up.

Seventeen or eighteen.

Tall.

Thin.

Badly in need of a haircut.

Green eyes peered out from under his disheveled hair. The brown leather bomber jacket he wore looked as though he had been wearing it for years. As if he had started wearing it when he was much younger with every intention of growing into it and now he finally had.

As was the fashion of so many people his age he wore a book-bag strapped to his shoulders. It was blue. There was a discoloration in the center where he had once placed a bumper sticker, but his father made him take it off. The cleaner he'd used to remove the gummy residue took out some of the color as well. He had written "Don't Panic" on the outside pocket. It was a thin homage to his favorite author Douglas Adams. It was also his current life motto. His previous life motto had contained four words, three of them profanities. That pretty much covers the reason his father made him take it off.

The book bag looked as though it was stuffed with half a dozen dictionaries, an industrial-size bag of M&M's, and a scale model of the Sears Tower in Chicago. In truth, nobody knew what he kept in the bag. He wore it so tightly strapped to his shoulders that the straps left marks in his skin. He wore it everywhere, convinced that only God could take it from him. He had mentioned this frequently to God, but so far, at least in Christian's mind, the Creator had been inattentive.

He violently flipped through the used paperback in his hand, searching. He devoured books, as if reading were a full-contact sport. Books seldom held together through a full reading. Duct tape was his favorite book cover. Christian's books were stained and marred. His parents long ago stopped buying him new books and, instead of giving him gifts, simply handed him some cash and dropped him off outside the used bookstore. Christian firmly believed that books communicated in sacred ways. If the Creator of the Universe wanted to pass a message on to him he could do it through the pages of any book he chose, not just the one with gilt-edged tissue paper and occasional red printing. So far, at least in Christian's mind, the Creator of the Universe had been inattentive.

Christian kept reading. He read books over and over, thinking maybe some new meaning would jump out at him "this time."

He had never felt more lost. If the eternal questions for his generation were "how do I get out of here?" and "where do I fit in?" Christian had been asking them for years. Which for him meant "forever." Which for him it pretty much was.

He threw the book into the yard and screamed at the sky. He screamed, "What do you want from me?"

When he heard no reply, he dropped to his knees in the grass and let his shoulders slump.

His mother and father came out of the house and picked him up off the ground. His mother tried to help him take off the backpack, but he shrugged off her hands and turned to them.

"I can't stay," he said.

"What are you talking about?" His mother began to fiddle with the apron in her hands as she often did when her son got like this.

"I've gone as far as I can go," Christian said. "There is no more for me here."

He started to shake and then fell forward. His father caught him, and his parents together led him up the stairs to his room. Again his mother tried to pry the book bag from his shoulders, but he jerked away from her and fell forward onto his bed, the weight of the backpack pressing his face into the mattress. He fell asleep and his parents left him there. They shooed his little sister away from the door and closed it behind them.

His mother, who had sat by his bedside when he was a child, did so again tonight. She worried and watched as he slept fitfully and drenched his sheets in his own sweat. His diploma sat on top of the dresser. It had not yet cooled down from the heat of his hand when he had received it only a few days ago.

In the morning, Christian stumbled down the stairs to the kitchen. Still wearing the book bag. Still wearing the same clothes. He flopped down at the table and put his face in his hands.

"Feeling better?" his mother asked. She was wearing her nothing-is-wrong-with-MY-son face. Her long history of ignoring problems until they went away was not serving her well this morning.

"Is this what a hangover feels like?" he asked. His mother laughed her oh-you-silly-boy laugh and busied herself in the kitchen.

Christian's father held the newspaper tighter and tighter. Until it was shaking.

Christian looked at his little sister and said, "Do you ever feel like your whole life is just fifty pounds of crap in a five-pound bag?"

His sister nodded. She had no idea what he was talking about. She spooned another spoonful of Frankenberry into her mouth and chewed as her brother mumbled and her mother hovered and her father vibrated.

His mother said, "I was hoping you would help me take some things over to the church bake-sale today and then maybe we could…"

"If I stay here," he said, "I'll never leave."

His mother began to fiddle with her apron again.

"There's more. I've never set foot out of this town. I've never been beyond the hill. I've never been anywhere…and if I stay…" he said again, this time looking at his mother, "I'll never leave."

His father, who felt he had listened to enough, said what he always said when his son started this. "Will you just snap out of it! *This* is all there is. There is no 'out there.' You don't need to go anywhere else or save the world or find yourself. This is *it*. You're upsetting your mother. Now sit down. Eat your breakfast. Today you can go hang out with those friends of yours and tomorrow we'll see about getting you a job in town."

Christian stood up and went to the door. His mother made a move to put a hand on his shoulder, but her husband said, "Let him go. He just needs to walk it off."

Christian's father believed that most problems could be solved by walking it off, working up a good sweat, or just snapping out of it.

Christian wandered the streets of his hometown. They called it the City of Ruin. Somehow, as he walked the streets today, the name fit better than ever.

He didn't "walk it off."

And he didn't go home again.

Ever.

Eventually he wandered into an empty parking garage. It was early morning and he walked up the ramps one by one until he was on the roof. He had been reading the book again and when he reached the center of the uppermost lot he looked at the sky again and shouted, "Okay! I'm here! What do you want from me?"

Things happen in great allegories differently than they do in the so-called "real" world. Suddenly, standing next to Christian was Preacher. Preacher had been the minister at the church Christian and his family attended when he was his little sister's age. Everyone called him just "Preacher" and Christian had always thought that was his name. Preacher knew how to do tricks with quarters and how to make paper airplanes that flew for miles. Christian had liked him a lot. He had died a long time ago.

"You're dead," Christian said, surprised by his own lack of surprise.

"Everybody had to be somewhere," Preacher said.

Preacher was only a little over five feet tall. He wore the same dark suit that he always wore. His hair, which consisted mostly of two white tuffets just above each ear, was combed neatly in place. His black glasses sat securely on his nose. He folded his hands and smiled at Christian as if he were the only man in the world completely at peace with himself.

"What seems to be the problem?" Preacher asked. His voice was full of quiet, gentle wisdom.

Christian pulled a book out of his jacket pocket and held it out to Preacher. "I'm spending my time looking for answers... instructions."

Christian shook the book. "Why doesn't God speak to me? I'm open to it. I read everything. He can speak to me through anything he wants, right? If I'm open to it... God will tell me. Right?"

"That's how God works?" Preacher said sarcastically. He gave himself a dope slap. "And all this time I've been... you know... praying and stuff."

Christian continued to stress. "Why don't I have a clue what God wants from me? I don't know where I'm supposed to go... what I supposed to do."

"What's keeping you here?" said Preacher.

Christian turned to show him the backpack.

"Ahhh," said the old Preacher. He leaned in and examined the way Christian was carrying the pack. He did not move to touch it. "Well," he said, "if that's how you feel, if that's how you *really* feel, then why are you hanging around here?"

The Preacher smiled as if he was holding back a birthday secret and reached down into the deep pockets of his black coat and brought up a Magic 8 Ball. Except this one was bright yellow and had a smiley face painted on it. He handed it to Christian, who shook it and turned it over. In the deep blue dye the triangle appeared. It read, "Haul Ass."

Christian looked at the Preacher and said, "Where do I go?"

The Preacher wrapped his arm around the boy's shoulder and pointed to the far distance. "Do you see that doorway?"

The young man squinted. "No. I don't see anything."

The Preacher put his hand on the back of the young man's head and turned it so they were looking in the same direction. With his other hand, he reached into his jacket pocket and pulled out a paper airplane. It was just like the kind he had made for Christian when he was a kid. He threw it. It soared over the buildings and disappeared into the distance. "Do you see that light?"

"Yes," said Christian. It was the first time his voice held a note of hope in days.

The Preacher said, "There. Go there. Walk toward that light. Keep it in your sights the whole time. When you get closer, you will see the door. When you get to the door, knock, and someone will be there to tell you what you are to do next."

Christian put the yellow smiling eight ball into his jacket pocket and from another pulled out his iPod. Placing the buds in his ears and hitting "play," Christian smiled at the Preacher, who smiled back. With that, the young man began to run. He ran toward the edge of the roof and, as if in a dream, jumped over and landed on the roof of the next building. He jumped over the next one, and the next, and then to the ground, where he didn't miss a step.

By this time, his family and friends were all searching for him and stood in shock as he suddenly ran by them. They shouted for him to stop. Some called him names. Some called him by his own. Others even threw things to trip him, but he kept running. Some even tried to follow, but Christian was singing along with the tunes on his iPod, so he would not be able to hear them call to him. He knew, somehow he just knew, that if he stopped running toward the light, even to talk with his family, the light would somehow dim and he would never find it again. Finally he settled down into a quick stroll. Confident and happy. He felt better than he had in a long time. He finally had something that he'd been missing. Direction.

As the music continued to ring in his ears, he felt something hit his back. A second object whizzed by his ear and he saw it was a small stone. His back was struck a second time and he knew someone was trying to get his attention. He took his eyes off the light for just a moment and turned to see who was behind him.

Trailing behind and tossing stones were two of his best friends from school. Plastic Man, named for the superhero who could bend himself in strange and bizarre ways. Plaz (the even shorter version of his nickname) could take his foot and, from a standing position, put it behind his head. Sometimes he wore a wristwatch on his ankle, and if you asked him what time it was, he would flip his foot up by his ear and read his watch.

Next to him was Bull. Christian had met Bull in the first grade. Bull had always been "big for his age." Once they hit high school, the coach for the football team had recruited Bull. Christian had spent a lot of time with Plaz in the bleachers watching members of the other teams take a run at Bull and simply bounce off as if they had run full force into a brick wall.

Christian stopped and laughed at how they both were panting from trying to catch up with him.

"Dude," Plaz said, but that was all he said because he was breathing so hard. He bent over and put his hands on his knees, then held up one finger as if to say, "One moment, my good man, whilst I catch my breath from this run you have so graciously led me on." However, all he could manage after a few seconds was another "dude."

Christian said, "Why are you guys following me?"

Bull, who was in better shape than the still panting Plastic Man, said, "To bring you home with us. Chris, you're not thinking straight. The whole town thinks you've gone over the edge. Your mother..."

"My mother thinks I've gone crazy and my father thinks I'm smoking something," Christian said. "Neither is true."

"Your old man is really pissed," Bull said. He reached down, grabbed Plaz by his shirt collar, and stood him up straight. "As of now, man, you're homeless."

"Come with me," Christian said.

"Dude?" Plaz said.

"Come with me," Christian said. "We'll make it a road trip."

"You have to come back from a road trip," Bull said.

"I'm never coming back to Ruin," Christian said. "Meteorites are going to drop out of the sky and fry everything. Come with me."

"Dude—" Plaz started to explain, but Bull cut him off.

"Chris, we're not going to leave. You're off your nut, man. You need to get some help. This is home. We live here."

Christian could see that Bull was too attached to his stuff...

his stuff in his room....

his stuff in his car....

his stuff in his garage....

his stuff in his school locker....

even his girlfriend Bull considered part of *his* stuff.

Christian said, "Bull, I have this feeling that where I'm going I don't need anything. I'm not taking anything with me because I'll find everything I need when I get there."

"Dude," Plaz said, pointing with his hand to his own back as if to say "what's that you're carrying."

"That's not my stuff," said Christian. "That's my...." Christian could not think of a proper word for the burden he carried all these years.

"Baggage?" Bull offered.

Christian looked at him. The word was close enough to the truth, but he turned his eyes away from his friend and looked back over the hill where he was headed. "Come with me," he said again.

Bull asked, "What's out there? What are you going after that you can't get here?" Bull gestured behind him at the City. Christian thought the gesture looked like a prize-model move on a game show. Christian had not noticed how ugly the City of Ruin looked until he saw it from this distance.

"What I am looking for," Christian said, "can't be held. It can't be pinned to your wall like a poster or plugged in. Every-thing—and I mean *everything*—you have down there is tem-porary. Eventually your car will rust out, your house will crumble, and the people will get old, dry out, and blow away." Christian held out the smiley face Magic 8 Ball. "What I'm looking at is the *only* thing in this world that is permanent."

"Dude?" Plaz asked, looking at his friend as if to say, "You know that's a toy, right?"

Bull looked at Christian in silence for a long time. He was trying to look as though he might actually be considering going along. But Christian could tell right away that deep down his friend was too afraid to leave. He was too afraid of the unknown and would rather take his chances in the City of Ruin.

"Screw you," Bull said, and then turned to Plaz. "Let's go. He's not coming back."

Bull turned to leave and got about ten steps back down the hill when Plaz said, "Uh...dude."

Bull turned around. "No way. You're not thinking of going with him. Plaz, are you nuts?"

Plaz stood between these two friends he had known since childhood. He had always been the peacemaker, always the one who could see both sides of an argument, always willing to go with the crowd. But now he had to make a choice.

"Come with me," Christian said.

"He's going to get you killed," Bull said.

Plaz held up his arms, shrugged a what-are-you-going-to-do gesture at Bull, and pleaded, "Dude?"

Bull turned and stormed off. Christian and Plastic Man watched him stomp back down the hill into the City of Ruin.

Chapter 2

As Christian and Plaz reached the top of the hill, they both paused. It was as if they both knew that the next step was the difference between going on and going back. Christian could see that Plaz wanted to at least have one last look at the City, so he put his hand on his friend's shoulder and edged him over the rise of the hill and down the grassy slope. They walked excitedly. This was the beginning of a journey. This was the first mile of the ultimate road trip, only without a car. Christian said, "How's life?"

Plaz said, "Duuuuuuuuuude." He said it like he had just taken a sip of iced tea after mowing his father's lawn in August. Christian knew exactly what he was talking about.

They walked in silence for a long time, still headed toward the light in the distance. Christian wasn't sure how long it would take to get there. He didn't know if he would still see the light after the sun went down. He didn't know if he would see it again in the morning if they stopped to rest. He reached into his jacket pocket for the 8 Ball.

"Dude," Plaz said, and motioned with his fingers to give the toy to him. Christian handed it to him.

"I had one like it when I was a little kid," Christian said. "I remember I always wanted it to be some kind of magic talisman or something. One day I broke it open to let the magic out."

Plaz looked at him.

"Yeah, I know," said Christian. "But I wanted to see. Turns out it's not water. It's blue dye. Stained the concrete on our front stoop. The stain is still there. This one..." Christian held out his hand and Plaz handed it back. "This one is special. It's going to speak to me." He drew a battered Bible from his jacket pocket and handed it to Plaz. Plaz looked at him and raised one eyebrow as he flipped through the pages without stopping.

"You've got to read it," Christian said. "It's good stuff. Beheadings. Sex. Death. Kings on top of palaces watching women bathe." Plaz looked at him as if he didn't believe it. "True," Christian said. "And the poetry, aw Plaz, there's this whole section in the middle that sounds like rock lyrics. Eventually we will get to the City of Light and then everything will be totally cool." Christian looked at Plaz. Plaz didn't say anything but Christian could tell he was listening.

"We're headed for a party," Christian said. "It's going to be a party like you've never seen before. Who's your favorite band?"

Plaz looked at him and gave him a sarcastic "Heh...Duu-uuuuu-de," as if it was obvious and he couldn't believe Christian didn't remember.

"Oh yeah," Christian said. "They'll be playing at this party."

"Duude!" Plaz said in amazement.

"The food, the girls, the music, the dancing. Every radio station in the world is going to be there giving out T-shirts and swag and you won't have to do any stupid stunts or answer trivia questions. They just give it to you."

Plaz kept walking. Christian could see his mind racing. "There's no pain," Christian said. He knew Plaz's family and its history. Plaz had spilled everything to him one night a few years ago. Plaz stopped and looked at him.

Christian walked as he talked. "No pain, no lies. No hiding things. You get to the door of the party and before the bouncer lets you in, he puts a hand on your shoulder and all of it washes away. The secrets are unimportant. The pain goes away. Everything is forgiven. It's like you get to start over from day one with a clean slate and no worries. Then they unhook the rope and let you walk in."

Plaz started to walk a little faster. Suddenly he stopped and in a worried voice said, "Dude?"

"It's okay," Christian said, taking the yellow Magic 8 Ball back from him. "This works like a backstage pass. We're in."

They walked along for another hour and soon found themselves walking along a dirt road that eventually became gravel, then pavement, then blacktop. No cars passed them as they walked. Up ahead they saw a rest stop. In the cool of the evening, they could read a flashing neon sign.

The sign, which may at one time have said "The Pit Stop," now simply said "The Pit S," due to the burned-out coils. Both of them were hungry and in need of a break. Christian and Plaz stood there looking at the building. It looked like the health department might have closed it down—if they had ever been there in the first place. "Piss and a Pepsi?" Christian asked.

"Dude," Plaz said, and they tapped fists.

Inside the Pit S a stench came from a garbage can that had not been emptied in a long time. Both Christian and Plaz were surprised to see how crowded the place was even though there were no cars outside. Christian and Plaz tried to make their way over to the men's room but were continuously thwarted by people pushing strollers, loud men with cell phones who were talking and not looking where they were going, large couples with larger trays of food that smelled a lot like the garbage can they passed on their way in.

After using the men's room, Christian noticed that his shoes were sticking to the floor. He did not want to know why. He saw Plaz standing in a long line with two bottles of soda pop in his hand. The woman standing in front of him was brushing her hair and Plaz was leaning away from each brush stroke as if something was coming off her scalp when she brushed. Plaz was about fifteenth in line and there were another fifteen behind him. At the front of the line, an angry man was talking both into his cell phone and to the girl behind the counter, who looked worried as she punched the buttons on the cash register one at a time. The machine would beep loudly and the girl would roll her eyes and start over.

Christian walked over and stood next to Plaz. He could tell that his friend was no longer excited about where they were going.

"Dude," Plaz said pleadingly.

"I know," Christian said, trying to sound understanding.

"Shoot," the cashier said. She punched the clear button and started again. The people in the line groaned.

Christian said, "They have one of those maps over there. I'll take a look and get a better idea of where we need to go from here."

As Christian wandered toward the map, he heard Plaz say something under his breath. Christian didn't hear what it was but he caught the gist. Plaz was not happy.

Standing in front of the map Christian looked for the YOU ARE HERE sticker, but there was none to be found.

He turned to look at Plaz, who had not moved forward, and shrugged an I-don't-get-it shrug.

At that moment, the baby in the stroller behind Plaz decided that the strained vegetables it had been fed for lunch were no longer part of his diet and projectile vomited them on the back of Plaz's pants and shoes. Plaz turned to look at the woman holding on to the stroller. She looked back and said, "What?"

Plaz shook what looked like liquefied peas off his pant leg and left the line. He walked over to Christian and slammed the two drinks down on the counter next to him. Christian met his eyes. He knew what was coming.

Plaz spoke two whole words: "Later, dude."

With that, he stormed out the door leaving a trail behind him that Christian imagined would not be mopped up for a long time. He was going to run after Plaz, but a voice said, "Can I help you?"

Christian turned and saw a small man standing next to him. The man's red hair was clipped close to his scalp, except for a thicker patch that ran along the top of his head. Christian guessed it may have been a Mohawk at one time but had been trimmed back to look professional. The little man wore a white, short-sleeved, buttoned-down shirt with black pants and an ugly tie. Pinned to his shirt pocket was a red plastic badge that said *May I Help You?* Beneath the white letters was a white box where someone had misspelled the word manager with a black magic marker—

MANAJER

"Nice place you have here," Christian said.

"It's a shithole," said the Manajer.

"You could clean it up," Christian said.

"Can't keep up with it," the Manajer said. "Every time we get more staff we get more people. I've got people working double shifts twenty-four seven and we just can't stay ahead of the crowd. Everyone who comes in acts as if we're their own personal toilet. Corporate office sends performance reviewers, they make suggestions, we implement them, and it all goes to crap immediately. You saw the sign?"

Christian nodded.

"Fixed it fifty times. Every time it burns out the same way and we wind up becoming "the Pits.""

A shriek came from the direction of the men's room. Dozens of people turned to look in that direction. Everyone except the

Manajer. He said, "This place will always be like this, no matter what we do, no matter how hard we work. This place was meant to be the Pits and it's going to stay that way."

"But it's your place," said Christian.

The Manajer shook his head. "I just work here."

Christian looked back at the map on the wall. "I was just trying to get my bearings and then I'll be on my way. I'm going to the City of Light and Preacher didn't give me great directions."

"Preacher sent you?" the Manajer asked.

"Yeah," Christian said.

"Small guy. White hair. Dark suit?" Christian nodded, glad that someone else knew who Preacher was.

"You're not going to find that path here," the Manajer said, pointing his thumb at the map. He tilted his head to one side as a gob of something green flew past his ear. "Let me show you where you need to go."

He walked Christian to the door, which looked as though it had grown even grimier since Christian and Plaz had arrived. "You need to keep going in the direction you were," the Manajer said. "Many people have been through here on the way to the City of Light. They left a trail. Everyone has followed that trail. The one who blazed it in the first place left footprints. Sometimes you can see them clearly. Other times you can't see them at all, and you just have to trust that you are on the right path."

Christian looked out into the parking lot. It was starting to get dark. He was tired, but he really didn't want to stay here. He thanked the Manajer, who looked at him with just a hint of envy in his eyes. Christian wanted to invite him to walk with him, but he knew the offer would be declined. The Manajer nodded and pushed the door open. Christian walked out into the night. From back at the rest stop he heard something crash against the dirty floor.

Elsewhere...

Plastic Man arrived back home. His friends and family bugged him and questioned him about the trip. Where had he gone? What had he seen? What had happened to Christian? Why had he come home and why had he left in the first place?

Plaz ignored these questions for a long time, but eventually, just to feel like he fit in again, began to mock Christian's journey just like the rest of the town.

Chapter 3

And so Christian found himself walking alone. He had no idea what was being said about him back home. He had no idea that his visit to the Pits had been videotaped by someone with a camera in her cell phone. He had no idea that websites and blogs had been posted taking bets about his progress and how people he had never met were writing "the real story" about him and his life. He had no idea that any of these things were going on. He simply walked down the road.

Eventually a pickup truck drove by him and slowed to a stop. Christian walked over to the passenger window and looked in. A small-framed man in a gray suit that matched the gray in his hair squinted and smiled at him. "Need a ride there, son? You look like you're about to fall down under that backpack. Why don't you throw it in the back of the truck and I'll drop you on up the road a stretch?"

Christian said, "No thank you. I can't take this off and there is only one person who can take it from me."

The man in the gray suit smiled. He had been reading the Internet and thought he knew all about Christian. He was already thinking of what he would write on his blog when he got home. "Who's that?"

Christian's half-smile disappeared. "Honestly, I'm not sure. I'm supposed to go to the doorway. The Preacher, he told me to take…"

"The Preacher?" the man in the truck said. "Heh heh. The Preacher always sends people on the hardest route possible. He thinks it builds character. So, you feel like you got your character built? Heh heh heh."

"Not lately," Christian said.

"Tell you what," the man said. "I can tell you a quicker way to get rid of the bag and you won't have to walk near as far. Whaddya say?"

"How can I be sure you know this easier way?"

"Cuz I been there, son," the man said. "I've picked up enough people on this road and they all have the same story. That the Preacher sent them and told them they had to take the hard way around when there's a perfectly good shortcut just over the hill."

Christian thought about the word shortcut. He had felt the skin of his shoulder chafing under the straps of his book bag and right now a shortcut sounded like a good idea.

"You got a family, son."

Christian nodded. He had not thought of them since he had left the City of Ruin. "To be honest, part of the reason I left was because I knew this weight that I'm carrying was cutting into their lives too. I couldn't do that to them anymore." Christian was surprised at how easy it was to talk to this man he'd never met.

The man in the gray suit nodded as he listened. Then he squinted and smiled again. "Okay, here's what you do. You see this hill. Right over this hill on the left here is a city called Moraltown. Nice place. Nice people. You'll see it as soon as you get over the hill. You'll want to go around the side and come in on Main Street. Get yourself on Main Street and look for the Law Offices of Legaleeze and Civilton. They's lawyers and they specialize in getting people's burdens removed, if you know what I mean. Heh heh heh. Hell, boy, once they got that thing off'n your back you might just want to consider suin' that there Preacher who sent you up the wrong path.

"You can get yourself a nice settlement. Buy yourself a big house there in Moraltown and have your family back in the City of Ruin join ya."

He laughed that strange laugh again and Christian wondered how the man knew where he had been from. "You tell Mr. Legaleeze that I sent you. My name is Orel. You got that?"

Christian said, "I got it. And I'll give it some thought."

"Thought? Hell, boy. I just gave you some of the best advice you're going to get and yer going to give it some thought?"

Christian stepped back from the truck and the man looked disgustedly at him and drove off, shooting bits of gravel at Christian as he watched the truck go.

Christian stood looking down the road and then looked off to the left. Over the hill was a shortcut. Over the hill was some-one who could take his burden immediately. Just a little over that rise was a nice little town where he could settle down and bring his family to live with him in a nice house. Chris-tian looked back over his shoulder to see if anyone else was coming and then marched toward the little hill. At the top of the hill, he saw the pretty little burg of Moraltown and smiled. He thought his journey was over before it even got too difficult. He smiled and started down the hill.

As he got closer to the city, Christian saw that a high wall surrounded the city. "Off to the left," he said, repeating the gray-suited man's instructions. Sure enough, off to the left was a path that led down the side of the hill. Christian fol-lowed it.

Within a few hundred yards the path had led him down below the edge of the city. The path also became quite narrow. Christian wondered what he would do if the path got any skinnier. He looked up and saw an intricate series of rotting boards that were propping up the edge of the buildings as they extended out over the land. It was as if each time one looked as though it might give way, someone added another board without thinking where it should go or removing the old ones.

Soon Christian realized that the path he was on was spiraling down to the bottom of a mountain, not leading him to the entrance to Moraltown. He had turned and faced the mountain, hoping that the book bag would not tip him backward and dump him down the side of the mountain.

As he eased himself along, he came to an edge where a gap in the path had appeared. Christian felt a vibration in the rock beneath his hand and looked up in time to see a series of the beams crack and begin to fall. He threw himself forward and landed on the path on the other side of the gap. The boards fell and crushed about ten feet of the path where he had just been standing. "Okay," said Christian. "Looks like we go forward."

Christian eased himself forward and downward. He was relieved to find that the path widened enough so that he could walk forward, but soon saw that at the bottom of the path sat a huge boulder. There was no going forward and there was no going back.

He looked up at the sheer face of the cliff. Far above him, he could make out the intricate web of beams that was holding up the City of Moraltown.

From the other side of the boulder in his path stepped Preacher.

"May I just ask," the Preacher said quietly, "what you would be doing here?"

"Uh…" Christian said, "I followed the path you told me about. And it led Plaz and me to this skanky rest stop. That's as far has he got, so I kept going on my own. This guy in a truck told me there was a shortcut to a city where they could take my backpack and I wouldn't have to walk all the way to the doorway. So I followed it."

"I see," said Preacher. "And how did that work out for you?"

Christian looked up at the path behind him and then at the boulder in front of him. The sudden alone-ness of the situation sunk in and he thought for a moment that he might scream. He took a deep breath and said, "Not so good."

The Preacher gently combed the white hair on the sides of his head with his fingers. He pushed up his dark glasses on his nose and then gave Christian a gentle dope slap upside his head. He put a hand on Christian's shoulder and said, "Here's where you went wrong."

"First. I gave you directions and you went for a shortcut. How'd that work out for you?"

Christian said, "Not so good."

The Preacher gave Christian another loving dope slap. Christian thought that one was a little harder than the first.

The Preacher said, "Second. You listened to a man who was not me. Did he once tell you that God was beside you? Did he once tell you that his way was God's way? Did he once say anything even remotely to do with being on a journey with God?"

"No. He didn't."

The Preacher sighed. He drew back to administer another dope slap but Christian saw this one coming and winced. The Preacher stopped and put his hand back on Christian's shoulder.

"Third. He sent you to a law firm in a place called Moraltown." At that moment, the Preacher pulled Christian out of the way, as another beam fell and landed with a thud in the spot where Christian had been.

"He told you," the Preacher continued, "that you could sue someone and they'd take your burden off you...."

Christian reached up and gave himself the dope slap this time. It was harder than the Preacher would have done, but the Preacher chuckled. "I think you're getting the idea."

Christian sighed heavily. "Is that it? Did I blow my one chance?"

The Preacher said, "Well, seems like you left the road that God wanted you on and followed the advice of an idiot. Hmm-mmmmmmmmmmmm."

"Won't happen again," Christian said hopefully.

"Come with me." The Preacher led Christian around the boulder that landed on the path. There was just barely enough room to scoot sideways while standing on his toes. Twice the Preacher had to help Christian keep his balance. When they got to the other side, Christian saw that there were two paths, one that looked clear and easy and one that looked rocky and treacherous.

"I'm guessing," said Christian, "that I'll be taking the hard way." There was a hint of sarcasm in his voice that made the Preacher look at him.

"And who left the path to begin with?"

"That would be me," Christian said. He adjusted the backpack on his shoulders and felt the straps chafe against his raw skin beneath his shirt. He started up the path.

Chapter 4

Eventually Christian made it back to the main road. There were no cars; there was no sign of the man in the pickup truck. The path had led him well beyond the City of Moraltown and he was once again alone.

Therefore, he kept walking. Each time his feet began to hurt he thought of the pain in his back and shoulders. He was pretty sure that beneath the straps of the book bag his skin was so raw that when the bag...*if* the bag were ever removed from him, his skin would crack and begin to bleed.

As he walked, he thought of the Preacher, he thought of the doorway, and he thought that maybe there should be some sort of magic words or special prayer that would insure his entering the doorway. There must be. They wouldn't tout it as this big holy doorway and not have a secret code or something, would they? He imagined the door itself. An archway made of polished stone; the door itself would probably be made of the finest metals with gold hinges. Yeah, a door like that. There's probably a secret knock. He began to compose a prayer greeting that he thought might be necessary when he got to the holy doorway.

Christian stayed walking in the direction the Preacher had sent him. Eventually the paved road turned to the left and Christian continued on a gravel road. The stones were harder to walk on, but he kept telling himself he was on the right road. The gravel road turned to dirt, and he began to wonder if maybe he had missed a sign when he left the pavement. But as he walked he saw a forest, and the dirt road (which was by now a dirt path) seemed to led right into the trees.

Christian ducked his head and walked into the cool dark wood. Following the path, he saw a clearing ahead. As he stepped through the clearing, he found himself in an open field. At the far end was a wall. In the center of the wall was a door. Not a big door, just an average door. Not an ornate door with gold hinges, but a wooden door with hinges that looked like they came from Home Depot. There was a stickie note on the outside of the door that said *Bell broken. Yell "Ding Dong."*

Christian knocked.

There was no answer.

After a few moments of embarrassment, he finally said, "Ding Dong."

A voice on the other side of the door said, "You'll have to say it louder. I'm not close enough to the door to hear you."

Christian looked around again and this time in loud a voice he said, "Diiiiiiiiiiiiiiiiiiinnnnnnnnnnnnggg. Dooooooooooonnn-nnnggg."

The singsong voice on the other side of the door said, "Whoooooooooooooo iiiiiiiiiiiiiiiiiis it?"

Christian cleared his throat and said,

"Oh thou gatekeeper would thee but let me in.
I am but a lowly traveler and a sinner and I
Uh.....wouldst enter thy doorway and be relieve-ed of
My burden. Open this door to me though I am not
Deserving of entrance to thine sacred places.
Let me but cometh
In and I will sing thee praises on high forever."

The door opened a crack and an eye peered out. It was the kindest eye that Christian had ever seen.

The voice said, "You are so full of crap."

Christian said, "I uhh...."

"Who sent you?" the voice asked.

"The Preacher," Christian said. "He told me to..."

At that moment, the door swung open and two very large hands grabbed Christian by the front of his shirt and yanked him in through the door.

"Hey!..." Christian said.

The man to whom the hands and the kind eye belonged threw both of them against the wall. He covered Christian with his massive frame. Christian peered out from beneath the big man's arms and saw six or seven arrows suddenly stuck in the door where he had been standing just a moment before. He heard a dozen others break against the stone wall.

The door swung closed on its own, and the man stepped away from Christian. He was easily 7 feet tall and had long white hair and beard. Beneath the beard was a kind smile. Christian saw that the kind eye that had peered at him through the crack was matched by another equally kind eye. The giant held out a massive hand. "Will," he said. "Will Goodman."

Christian watched his own hand disappear into the big man's. "Christian," he said. "What the heck was that?"

Will Goodman said, "Neighbors. We don't get along. Something about a property line."

"So, they try to kill you when you open the door?" Christian said, unbelieving.

Will Goodman smiled. "No, boy. They were trying to kill you."

"What did I do?" Christian asked.

"You're on this journey, aren't you? Neighbors like mine don't want to see anybody get where they are going. They take it personally."

"I understand," Christian said. But he really didn't. He was feeling both lucky and terrified at the same time.

The old man and the young man both turned as they heard another arrow glance off the other side of the door. Will Goodman said, "You're alone?"

Christian nodded. "I had two friends from school who started out with me, but they didn't stay very long."

The older man nodded but the kindness did not leave his eyes. "Family?"

"Back in the City of Ruin," Christian said. "To tell the truth, I think they're mostly glad I left."

Will Goodman nodded again and put his arm around the boy's shoulder. "You say the Preacher sent you?"

Christian nodded. "He said you would be able to tell me where I go next."

Will Goodman turned and lowered a huge wooden latch on the door. "Anywhere but back," he said. "Come with me. You're hungry." It wasn't a question.

A few moments later Christian and Will Goodman were in the old man's kitchen. He had made coffee and grilled cheese sandwiches. They stood at the counter and ate as Christian told him the stories of his travels. Of the man at the Pits who said he could never leave, of his detour down the path, and of nearly being killed by the falling beams beneath Moraltown.

"The old man in the truck steered you back-assward, didn't he?"

Christian nodded and finished his sandwich.

"Lying bastard," Goodman said. "Come here. You help me with the dishes."

There weren't many dishes, but they did them together. Christian remembered how he used to help his mother with the dishes after supper. Goodman's words rang in his ears—

"Any way but back."

"This is my favorite part of the day," Goodman said. Christian looked up and saw the man gazing out the window above the sink. Christian looked and saw a beautiful sunset. "Do you see that path?"

Christian looked. The evening sun illuminated a long path that seemed to vanish at the horizon. "Yes, sir," he said.

"There was this teacher who cleared that path, as did the prophets before him. It was laid there by the Creator of the Universe. It's as straight as if he laid it out with a ruler. That's your path. Stay tonight. Tomorrow you can start down that path."

Christian suddenly remembered the detour the man in the pickup truck had sent him on. "Is it hard?"

Goodman put the last dish into the cupboard. "Yes," he said. "But you will always know you are on the right one because it is straight. If you find yourself on a winding path, you've gone the wrong way. Understand?"

Christian nodded. He felt the strap on his shoulder and tried to ease his thumb under it because it was itching. He thought about asking Will Goodman about the pack but Goodman seemed to know what he was thinking.

"Just a little while longer. Just a little longer and you will come to a place called the Rescue Mission. Once you get there, your baggage will fall off all by itself."

Christian recognized the feeling in his chest. It was hope. He hadn't felt it since he'd left the City of Ruins.

"Tomorrow you will start off bright and early," Goodman said. "You will find a little stand by the side of the road."

"And?" Christian asked.

"Do you like jelly?" Goodman said, and he started to giggle.

Christian followed Goodman into the next room. There was a

large sofa and a pillow with a Scooby Doo pillowcase just like the one Christian had had as a child. Goodman went to a cupboard and came back with a thick blanket. "You'll want to turn in soon."

Christian didn't want to turn in. He had so many questions, but as he stared at the pillow and held the blanket close to him, he found that all he wanted to do was lay on that large couch and sleep.

Chapter 5

Christian started out early.

Will Goodman had given him a cup of strong coffee in a well worn travel mug that said "Javahhhhhhhhhhhhhh." Most of the h's were worn away. Christian stayed on the straight path just as he was told to do. He had started just after sunup and by early morning the heat was becoming oppressive. Several times Christian saw a second path just 50 yards to his left that was in the shade of the mountain. He thought several times about simply walking on the shaded path until the sun reached it as well but he managed to make himself stay where he had promised Goodman that he would stay. It was just past midday when he saw the roadside stand that Will Goodman had told him about.

As he got closer, he could smell the fresh fruits and vegetables. There were hand-painted signs for "Fudge" and "Peanut Brittle." Behind the plywood counter in the shade of a canvas tarp sat a woman in the largest, brightest colored hat that Christian had ever seen.

"Well my goodness gracious! Don't you look like you've been walking all day." She stood and without asking reached into a cooler and pulled out a large plastic jug of tea. She set it on the counter and said, "Here, you give me that." She took the travel mug from Christian's hand and looked at it. "You got this from Will Goodman, didn't you?"

Christian said, "Yes ma'am."

She smiled wider and said, "Well, somebody is on a journey, aren't they." She took the cup over and turned on a faucet that was coming up out of the ground. She rinsed out the mug and filled it with cold tea. "Here," she said. "It's sweet tea."

Christian took it, sipped, and felt the coolness of the dark brown liquid, as it seemed to cool his entire body. He felt it down to the tips of his fingers. The woman in the floppy hat smiled the way a cook smiles when she watches you eat a slice of her pie or taste her biscuits. "It's a good batch," she said.

Christian didn't have to say anything in return. He simply said, "Oooooohhhhhhhhhhhhhh."

"You can look around if you like," she said. "Any friend of Will Goodman's is welcome here. Would you like a cookie?"

Christian said that he would, and from a box behind her, the woman produced a thick chocolate chip cookie the size of a small pizza. She held it in a piece of wax paper and gave it to him. Christian took a bite and closed his eyes again. The woman smiled.

"Will Goodman said you can teach me things that I will need to know for my road trip to the City of Light," Christian said.

The woman came around from behind her counter and gently touched Christian's face. Her hand drifted to the pack. Just her light touch on the shoulder where the pack met his skin made him wince. "It won't be much longer," she said. "You have things you must learn first."

She led him to a rack of postcards. It was the kind of rack you would expect to find in any tourist shop along any highway. Bikini-clad girls or a map of the state and *Hello from Florida* in bright sunny letters. But this was not just "any" tourist stop. Christian looked and saw that every postcard was a drawing of Jesus. Some looked like pictures from comic books. Others reminded Christian of the artwork he had seen in his Sunday school books as a child. There was one that looked like stained glass that showed Jesus carrying a lamb. There was another with deep rich colors as if it were an oil painting. That one showed Jesus beaten and bloody and hanging from the cross. There was one of Jesus surfing. There was one of Jesus holding children in his lap and telling them a story. There was one of Jesus angry. Jesus crying. Jesus laughing. Jesus looking surprised. Jesus looking somber as he held up his hand in what looked like the Boy Scout salute. Christian slowly spun the rack to see if there was anything other than Jesus postcards.

"Did you notice?" the floppy hat woman asked.

"Notice what?" Christian said.

"You didn't notice," she replied. She took five postcards at random, and put them in Christian's hand. "Look at them again and tell me when you notice."

She went back around to the other side of the wooden counter and began to straighten the peaches.

Christian looked at the postcards in his hand and the hundreds that were on the rack. He turned them over and back and saw nothing unusual other than they were all different and they were all of Jesus. He began to grow frustrated. Was this his first test? Was he failing it already? "I don't know what I'm supposed to notice," he said.

"He's looking at you," she said.

Christian looked again. Every postcard in his hand showed Jesus looking at him. In every postcard on the rack, Jesus was looking at him. The angry Jesus, the laughing Jesus, the weeping Jesus, the surfing Jesus, they were all looking straight out of the postcard and directly at him.

"I don't understand," Christian said.

"You aren't alone," she said. "You are never alone. He is always with you. When you are laughing, he is laughing with you. When you are grieving, he is grieving with you."

Christian became irritated. "If he is always with me why has he not taken this stupid backpack? It's been stuck on me like glue since I can remember. If he is all about love, why do I have to keep carrying this? Why am I risking my life for him?"

The woman with the floppy hat did not smile this time, but there was still love in her eyes.

"Child," she said, "he never promised you he would. He only promised that he would always be with you."

Christian did not look at her. He put the postcards back in the rack. It was not the answer he wanted. He scowled. "I don't understand."

She said, "Come with me."

Christian walked around to the other side of the counter. With great kindness she took his hand and led him over to a table that was filled with canning jars of homemade jelly. There were all kinds of colors and all kinds of flavors. Each one was labeled with a handwritten sticker telling what was within.

She reached to the back of the table, pulled out a pint-sized jar with a gold-colored lid, and put it in his hands.

Christian looked and saw that the jelly inside was gray. It looked as though the fruit inside was rotting. He saw what looked like half a roach. He saw something else that he was pretty sure was still moving, but it disappeared in the chunky rancid-looking muck. There was no label. "What is it?" Christian asked.

"Mankind's soul," she said. Then she handed him another jar. This one looked like strawberry jam. It was a deep red color and there were large pieces of berries. It made Christian's mouth water.

"And what's in this one?"

"Grace," she said. "The love we get from the Father whether we deserve it or not."

The woman turned and lifted a small baker's cloth. Beneath were a dozen or more fluffy golden-brown biscuits, each one the size of Christian's fist. "Open them."

"Both of them?" Christian asked. He was sensing what she was going to do and the idea made his stomach turn.

"Well of course," she said.

Christian opened both jars. The smell from the gray dirty jar made him turn his head. The woman pulled a spoon from her apron and said, "We're going to take just a little from one and put it in the other. What will happen?"

Christian said, "A little from this one," he said, holding out the gray jar, "will ruin this one," he said, holding out the other.

"And visa versa?" she asked.

"A little from the grace jar isn't going to make a lot of difference over here."

"You would think that would be true," she said. Her tone reminded Christian of his favorite teacher, who had stayed late every day to help him with his math homework.

She took a spoonful of the wonderful-smelling strawberry jam and dripped it into the jar where things had been crawling. Christian watched as the gray matter in the jar suddenly began to transform. The foul smell went away and the color turned from grayish to a red as deep as the red in the other jar. Even the filthy glass seemed to get clean all on its own.

"Now," she said, "it's not enough to just change the contents of the jar. You have to have some faith to go with it. She took a fresh biscuit, spooned some of the jelly from the changed jar, put it on a biscuit and handed it to him.

Christian took it. He had seen what HAD been in the jar. He had seen the floating bugs. He had seen the slithery thing that crawled away from the light when he turned the jar in his hand. He had seen all of that.

He looked into the kind eyes of the woman and popped half of the biscuit in his mouth.

It was the most wonderful thing he had ever tasted.

"And?" she asked.

"Iss wunnerfull!" he said with his mouth full.

She smiled. "Grace makes it clean. But you have to have faith to go with it. Faith is what makes the soul ready for God. Now come with me."

Christian shoved the rest of the biscuit in his mouth and allowed himself to be led by the hand. She led him past the roadside stand to a small cottage. She peeked in the window, smiled and motioned him to come closer. "My grandsons," she said.

Christian looked in and saw two boys, both about 8 or 9 years old. They were sitting at the kitchen table. One was reading and the other was working on what looked like a model airplane. On the stove was a huge pot. Christian could smell the jelly cooking from outside.

The boy building the model kept looking up from his work and at the pot on the stove. He got up and walked toward it.

"You have to wait," said the other. "Grandma says it's not ready."

"He's curious," said Christian.

"He's a little dope," said the woman. "I told him a hundred times. It's not jelly yet. You have to wait, seal it in a jar and let it sit for awhile, but he's so impatient."

The boy staring at the pot on the stove suddenly reached up and put his finger in the bubbling liquid. He howled in pain and began to dance around.

"Saw that coming," the woman said, and she started for the front door.

"Graaaaaaaaaaaaaaammmmmmmmmmmmmaaaaaaaaaaaaaaaaaaaaaa!" he cried.

Christian watched her from the window as she gently brought the boy over to the sink, where they ran cold water on the child's finger. He whimpered and cried. When she spoke to him, her voice was soothing enough, but her words were firm.

"I told you what would happen, didn't I?"

The boy nodded his head.

"I told you the jelly wouldn't be ready for awhile, didn't I?"

The boy nodded again.

She kissed his burned finger, kissed the top of his head, and guided him back to his chair. She stirred the bubbling jelly with a long wooden spoon and then kissed both boys on the top of the head and said, "Stay out of my jelly and I'll make you lunch in just a little bit."

She went outside and Christian was waiting for her. "Guess he learned his lesson," Christian said.

She rolled her eyes and said, "Hardly. Happens all the time."

Christian looked at her. "I don't understand."

She looked at him. "People all over the world are so obsessed with having things now...right now...don't want to wait...just give it to me now now now."

Christian nodded. He had seen this himself.

"A little patience," she said, "just a little patience and they'll have everything. But no, you can't tell some people that. No matter how many times you tell them not to they keep going back and sticking their finger in the hot pot."

"And they get burned," Christian said.

"And they get burned," she confirmed. "People walk around this life wailing 'Grandmaaaaaaaaaa, I burned my finger.' They want all their rewards up front. No matter how many times you try to tell them about how God has it all planned out. God has wonderful things in store for you. Just let it happen in HIS time and NOT yours. Nevertheless, people don't listen. They want it all now."

"And then they get burned," Christian said again.

"Again and again. Now come with me."

Once again she took him by the hand and led him behind the little cottage. There, a small frazzled man was filling a giant water balloon. He set it gingerly on the ground and tied it closed. Then, lifting it with two hands he carried it over to what looked like a giant catapult. He set the balloon in the pouch, which was already soaking with repeated tries. The man rushed over and checked a set of blueprints that were laid out on a table. He ran over and adjusted something on the catapult.

"How's it going today, George?" she called out.

He looked up and saw the woman and Christian. She was still holding Christian's hand. The man she had called George smiled. "Today is the day!" he said.

"For what?" Christian whispered.

"Ask him," she said.

"Today is the day for what?" Christian called to George.

"The day I put out the sun." With that, George pulled a lever and the catapult fired the massive water balloon at the sky. All three of them stood and watched as it flew higher and then finally plummeted back to earth about 50 yards away. It splashed as it hit the ground. Christian stared and saw that the field was covered in broken balloon pieces as if not only George but also his ancestors had been firing balloons at the sun for generations.

"Maybe next time, George," she called. She led Christian by the hand and they walked away leaving George to his impossible task.

"What's my lesson here?" Christian said.

The woman looked at him from beneath her floppy hat. "You can't put out the sun."

"Right," Christian said.

"You don't understand," she said. "You can't put out the *son*."

Christian nodded.

Finally, she took his face in her hands and spoke to him as if she was speaking to a child. "Son. As in s-O-n. Not s-U-n."

"Oh," Christian said.

"Exactly," she replied. "We have more things to see."

She led him from the back of the house to the front where her roadside stand stood. A very large man stood next to the cooler where the woman had given Christian some tea when he arrived. "His name is Francis," the woman said. "Works for me." Francis was the biggest man that Christian had ever seen. He was broad-shouldered and very tall. He stood with his arms crossed and one foot on the cooler. Around him a group of men were staring at him and at the cooler. One of the men suddenly charged the cooler and Francis caught the man in midstride and easily threw him through the air back toward the crowd of the other men. He landed with a thud and slowly struggled to a sitting position, where he remained. Two others charged, one after the other. Francis caught the first and simply shoved him into the second, and both went down. They crawled over to where the first charger was sitting and sat with him, looking dejected. A fourth man, this one smaller than the rest, ran. Francis batted him away as if he was a bug in his face. The little man rolled and finally came to a stop. "Anybody else?!" Francis boomed.

Those still standing took a step back. Those who were sitting looked away. However, the fourth man, the little one who had been batted away, easily stood. Francis looked at him, surprised. The little man charged again. Francis caught him again and tossed him away like he was weightless. The man hit the ground again.

"I don't underst..." Christian started.

"Shhhh!" said the woman. "Let's see what happens next."

"*Come onnnnn!*" Francis said, and beat his chest with his fists. "Gimme Somebody!"

At first no one moved, and then the little man who had been slapped away twice before stood again. He wiped the blood from his nose and looked at Francis. Francis smiled and cracked his knuckles. The man charged. This time Francis caught him by the neck and lifted him off the ground.

"Francis!" the woman called. All eyes turned toward Christian and the woman with the floppy hat. "That will be enough," she said. "Give him a drink."

Obediently Francis set the man down and brushed the dirt from his clothes. He bent over the cooler and pulled out a bottle of ice-cold soda pop. He even offered the man a chunk of ice for the cut on his nose.

The woman pulled Christian away. "I think I've to get this one on my own," he said.

"Good," she said. "You're almost ready."

They walked together back to the house. It was getting late in the day. She opened the back door. The boys were watching television, but the grandson who had burned himself before kept sneaking out to the kitchen to peek into the cooking pot. Christian guessed it was only a matter of time before he stuck his finger in again.

She led him toward a back hallway. In the farthest part of the house was a small room. She opened the door, and in the center of the room was a man. He was weeping. He wore a suit that shined so brightly Christian thought it would glow in the dark. The lapels of the jacket were trimmed with fake diamonds. His hair was thick and brown and Christian supposed immediately that it was a wig. The man held his hands up in the air and shook his head sadly. He cried, "I am so so sorry, my Father. I have disappointed you again and again."

Christian looked at the woman and she nodded. "Go ahead."

"What did you do?" he asked the man in the bright suit.

"I have sinned against my Father!" the man cried. "I have crucified my God all over again. I have given myself to the worst of my sinful sinful nature." The man turned away from them. Christian watched as he not-so-subtly withdrew a small bottle from his coat pocket. He put a few drops of liquid in each eye, and then, turning back around, allowed saline tears to flow freely from his eyes. "Oh eternity. Eternity. How can I cope with the misery?"

Christian looked back at the woman and she asked, "Ready to go?"

Christian nodded.

"Good," she said. "One more stop."

As they left the room and began walking out of the house Christian said, "I don't understand that one at all."

The woman smiled and said, "Not many people do. Some people just get a lot more enjoyment out of being miserable than they do out of being happy."

"That doesn't make sense," Christian said.

"Ya think?"

They went out the front door. A large tour bus had stopped by the Roadside Jelly Stand. People had stopped and were carrying jars of jelly and cookies in their hands. A bus driver stepped off the bus. He was dressed all in white and his cap was made of gold. "Let's go, folks!" he shouted. "All aboard!" The sign on the front of the bus said "City of Light."

"Should I be getting on the bus?" Christian asked hopefully.

"That's not part of your journey," she said. "You're going a different way."

As the people lined up to get back on the bus, Christian noticed that a man at the back of the line was carrying a suitcase. It was a large suitcase and he wasn't just carrying it, he was clutching it to himself. As he got close to the door the bus driver said, "Where did you get that? Didn't I take that from you once before?"

As the bus driver reached for the bag, the man backed away, pulling the suitcase closer, like a child clinging to a blanket. "Give it to me now," the driver said firmly. "You know you don't need it anymore." He grabbed the bag, but the man pulled it away and ran toward the road. The bus driver chased him and finally tackled the man to the ground.

"What's in the bag that's so valuable?" Christian asked.

"It's not valuable," the woman in the hat said. "It's all the pain, all the disappointment, all the anger he's collected over the years."

They had reached the wooden counter where Christian had first met the woman in the floppy hat. She began to pack a paper sack full of jelly jars, biscuits, and cookies. Christian looked at the man who was still wrestling with the bus driver. He broke free and ran down the road. The driver brushed the dirt off his white suit and ran after him.

"Why would you want to keep all that so close to you?"

"Why indeed," she said.

She handed him the paper sack and kissed his cheek. "Time to go."

Chapter 6

Christian walked the path for several hours. He stopped once or twice to rest and try to adjust the book bag on his back. He had barely noticed it while he was at the roadside stand. He hadn't noticed it at all when the woman with the floppy hat had shown him the bizarre sights. But now...now it was hurting him worse than ever. The road took a steep incline and he had to lean forward to keep from falling backward. At the top of the incline there was a grassy hill that veered off from the left-hand side of the road. There was a deep but narrow ditch and then a rocky grade. At the top of the grade was a cross. There was no light show, no fanfare, no pre-recorded choir of angels singing an "Ahhhhhhhhhhhhhh." It was just one lone cross standing off to the side of the road, so out of place that you could not help but notice it.

Christian stared at it for a very long time. It was off the path. Should he go off the path? It was a cross. It must be safe. He listened for a voice or some sort of invitation, but there was nothing, nothing audible at least. The more he stood there the more it seemed like the cross was actually "pulling" him toward it. Christian stepped off the road and began walking toward the rocky grade. He jumped the ditch and felt the straps of the bag dig into his shoulders when he landed on the other side.

He began to climb the rocky grade. It wasn't impossible, but he was practically on all fours, feeling even more like a pack animal. When he reached the top of the grade he stood there in front of the cross. It was made of two-by-fours held together with bolts and nuts. It was simple and rugged and meant for lots of wear and tear rather than any sort of decoration. Christian had seen crosses standing in threes off the side of the road when they drove through the South on family vacations. This one was different. He looked around for a plaque or a bundle of dried memorial flowers, but there was nothing but the cross. It was taller than he was, with nothing distinctive whatsoever. Yet he had the strangest sensation that the cross…well…it wanted to hug him.

Gently, Christian reached out and put his hand on the cross. He felt a sudden energy sweep through him. It started in the tips of the fingers in the hand where he touched the wood and then shot up through his arm and through his whole body. It wasn't hot, like touching a stove, and it wasn't electric, but the sudden jolt vibrated him down to his toes.

He jerked his hand back and looked at his fingertips.

Something fell to the ground in front of him. He picked it up. It was the buckle from the strap on the book bag. He watched as the metal buckle dissolved in his hand like rapidly melting ice. It felt cool to the touch, puddled, and then vanished completely. What happened next happened so quickly that he actually had to stop and tell himself what had happened. He heard the sound of the other buckle popping and then in about a second and a half the book bag dropped from his back with a sound that reminded him of ripping Velcro. The book bag fell to the ground. It rolled down the rocky grade and bounced once…twice…and finally dropped into the ditch. His first inclination was to grab for it, but he jerked his hand back as if he just realized that the burner was hot.

Christian looked at the spot where it had dropped into the deep ditch. He felt suddenly lost. It was gone. That simply. It was gone. No otherworldly giant hand had come down and yanked it off him. No army of angels had swooped down to carry it away. The buckles dissolved like butter melting and the book bag fell off of him.

The weight was gone.

The baggage was gone.

Christian rolled his shoulders backward to double-check. The bag was gone. He reached behind him with his hand and felt only the back of his leather bomber jacket. The bag was gone.

Christian dropped to his knees and began to weep. His skin felt empty. His body felt free, and at the same time it was like having a limb amputated. It was like the sudden death of someone close to you. He fell to the ground and rolled over on his back. He could not remember the last time he lay flat on his back. He could not remember what the ground felt like this way. He could not remember a time when he did not have the weight on his back. Now it was gone and he was weeping.

A voice said, "Peace."

Christian turned. Three shining beings were standing between him and the cross.

"My bag is gone," he said. He had to tell someone.

"You're welcome," one of the beings said. "Now you are ready to begin."

"Begin?" Christian asked.

The first being, the one who had spoken, shimmered in light. It was as if the being itself was not there. All the shadows one would see on another person were there, and they were glowing in light. The being reached out and touched Christian. Immediately his dirty, ratty, secondhand clothes became brand-new. They were still the same clothes, but crisp and new, right down to his socks and underwear. His Converse All Stars were brand-new, black with shiny white laces. The only thing that had not changed was his bomber jacket. Christian was glad of this. It had taken him years to break it in. Christian ran a hand through his hair and his fingers felt clean. He was shaven and scrubbed and his hair was freshly cut. All of this happened in a matter of seconds.

The second shining being touched him and he felt a quick burning sensation on his wrist. When he looked down there was a fresh tattoo on his wrist. It was a music staff and beneath that were the words *The Lord's.*

Christian was about to say something when the third being held out what should have been a hand and gave Christian an iPod with a set of earbuds. "You're going to need it," a voice said. Christian looked at the iPod. It was shimmering white in color. He put the buds in his ears and he hit the "play" button. The music that filled his ears was unlike anything Christian had ever heard. It was like heavy-metal music played on acoustic instruments. The guitar player seemed to be using his guitar as a drum and the drummer sounded like he was playing a slinky. Their voices melded in a joy that practically lifted Christian off the ground.

Oh them lions they can eat my body
but they can't swallow my soul.
They keep on tryin' to crash my party
but they can't get control.

He turned and ran down the hill. He found that without the weight on his back he felt as light physically as he did spiritually and emotionally. His steps took him into the air. His jumps felt like he was flying. The music in his ears lifted him.

With one jump he soared over the ditch where his burden had fallen. He didn't look down. He didn't even notice it. He jumped into the air and did a full forward flip before gracefully landing on his feet. He twirled and spun his way to the bottom of the hill and without a second thought began to walk along the path again. Feeling as if he were lighter than air, his steps took him yards at a time.

*****

Over the crest of the steep hill Christian looked down and saw a car stuck in the mud off to the side of the road. It looked as though it had been there for a very long time. There were three young men about Christian's age. One was sleeping on the hood, one was on the roof, and the last was on the trunk with his feet propped up on the roof. They were all covered in mud.

From where he was standing he could see that someone had written on the windows of the car in white paint, like high school students do when they are about to graduate. The side window of the car read "Lazy, Stupid, and Guesswork." The other window simply said "ROCK!!"

Christian ran down the hill feeling the wind in his hair. When he reached the bottom he pulled the buds out of his ears and looked at the three young men. "Do you need help?" he asked.

The one who was lying on the hood looked up and said, "Nah, thanks man. We got it."

The one on the roof raised his hand in a thumbs-up sign.

The third yawned but did not move. Christian supposed that this was the "Lazy" from the window, but he really had no idea.

"I can help," Christian said. "You don't want to hang around here all day. Best to keep moving. Satan prowls like a roaring lion seeking whom he will devour. I heard that in a song once."

The first one raised his head again and looked around. "Yeah, got it man. Thanks for the advice."

When Christian saw they really didn't want his help, he shrugged his shoulders and moved on.

*****

As Christian continued along he noticed that the road was lined on either side with large white bricks. The further he walked the higher the bricks stood on either side of the road. Within half an hour the footpath was between two very high walls on either side. The increase was so slow that Christian had barely noticed when the walls on either side of the path were over his head. Strangely, Christian found a sort of comfort in the high walls. He could look up and see the stars and know that nothing could come from off-path and kill him.

As he walked he heard voices. He stopped in his tracks to see where the voices were coming from. Suddenly he saw a foot appear over the wall. Then a hand. Finally, the lower half of a body climbed over and the rest of the person as well dropped in front of Christian. "Oh. Well, hello my good man." The stranger who had climbed over the wall was dressed in a full tuxedo. The man straightened his jacket and adjusted his tie and the flower in his lapel. "Delighted to meet you." He gave a small bow and extended his hand. Christian shook it.

"HEY!" a voice from above him said. "Oh, do pardon me," the man in the tux said and began to assist a second person down from the high wall. The new member of the group turned and looked at Christian when he got his feet under him. Christian stepped back. The man had two faces. One on either side of his head. Christian tried to pretend he didn't notice and held out his hand. The man with two faces shook it and then turned to his companion. "Thanks a lot for the help."

"Sorry, I was chatting with this young man. I rather hadn't expected anyone to be here."

Christian said, "Are you going to the City of Light too?"

The men looked at each other. "Why yes," said the more formal one. "Yes, we are."

Christian looked a little worried. "Why didn't you come through the gate?"

"This way was quicker," said one of the two faces.

"Then you didn't see the woman with all the jellies, or the old man, or even the Preacher?"

The two men (with three faces total) looked at each other like they were saying, "What the heck is he talking about?"

"This way was quicker," the man with two faces repeated.

"Yes," said Christian, "but 'the way' is more than 'a way.' It's also lessons for what we will face as we walk to the City of Light."

"As long as we get to the city. Who cares how we get there?"

"But," Christian said, "the destination is only half of the experience. The other half is what happens when you are actually going." He said this and made air quotes with his fingers around "going."

"We're going," the man with two faces said. He mocked Christian by repeating his air quotes. "You can stay here or you can walk with us."

The three of them set off together. Christian tried several times to make conversation, but eventually chose to listen to the iPod the shiny angel had given him The music gave him much comfort as he walked along. And without the bag strapped to his back, he didn't feel tired at all.

Chapter 7

The three of them walked together along the narrow path with the high walls for a long time. The man in the tuxedo and the man with two faces chatted occasionally back and forth and, for the most part, completely ignored Christian.

Christian was content to listen to the music device that the shimmering one had given him. So far it had only played music. It had not given him any instructions and he wondered what the shimmering one had meant when he said, "You're going to need it."

The path started to turn downhill, and the three young men moved quicker with the slope. Christian was soon at a full jog when he noticed the walls on the sides of the path were getting closer. "No, the walls aren't moving," he thought. "The path is getting narrower."

All three of them could see the bottom of the hill. They could see where the walls stopped but they could not see what was beyond. Tux and Two-Face (as Christian had come to think of them, because they had not shared their names) ran ahead. Christian kept his pace, and when he reached the bottom of the hill, he saw the path had opened onto an open field. From this point all three of them saw that the path they had been on diverged into three. The straight path continued on, though it was now a dirt path marked by rocks. There was a wrought iron arch with black letters that read "Hill of Difficulty."

"That's cheery," said Tux.

Two other paths diverged in separate directions.

Tux said, "I would suppose that all three paths meet up on the other side of the hill. We should each take a separate way. Might be one of those riddles. One of the paths has a great treasure and if we each take a separate route…we'll be sure to find it."

Two-Face nodded his agreement.

Christian said, "Look, this guy I know—the one who sent me this direction in the first place—said to stay on the straight and narrow path no matter what."

"The 'guy' you know," Tux said. He mocked Christian's air quotes again even though Christian had not made any. Tux then smirked at Two-Face.

"He's been right up until now," Christian said.

"Look, kid," Tux said (even though he wasn't that much older than Christian). "You do what you want. We're going in separate directions and you can meet us at the end or you can take the middle or you can turn around and go the hell home. I don't care. We're going to find whatever is hidden and we're going to split it between us on the other side. Fifty-fifty."

Tux held up his fist to Two-Face. Two-Face bumped it with his own and the two of them ran off in separate directions.

Christian stood alone and watched until each of them had disappeared around the side of the hill.

Christian put his ear buds back in his ears and started up the straight and narrow path in front of him. The path was steep and hard going but the music in his ears helped.

*****

Tux walked quickly down the path he had taken. He once looked back and saw Christian taking the harder path up the center of the hill and he laughed to himself. He took off his tuxedo jacket and folded it over his arm. It was warm, but at least his path was smooth and straight. Soon he came to a thick forest. The trees were dense, but the path was clearly visible. He walked in and made several long winding turns until he came to a place where the path seemed to simply fade away into the leaves. "I missed my turn," he said to himself.

Turning around, Tux wandered back down the path, but soon found he wasn't walking on a path at all. He looked around, but there was nothing. No path. No break in the trees. A light that was slowly fading in the sky. He pushed forward hoping he would find the path again, but he didn't. He began to panic, and then to run, but this got him nowhere. He caught his jacket on a tree branch and it was jerked out of his arms. He let it go. He could get another one. The more he wandered, the thicker the branches and brambles seemed to grow around him. He was fairly certain that the forest itself wasn't really getting thicker. The trees were moving closer. There was a huge tree in front of him, behind him, and on either side. He was pretty sure he would have remembered stepping into a spot that was closely surrounded by trees. The last thought in his head was, "Yeah, I don't think trees are supposed to do this."

Two-Face jogged on the path he had chosen. It was important to him to be on the other side of the hill first. He wanted to beat his friend in the tuxedo, but mostly he wanted to beat Christian. He soon noticed the air was getting thinner and colder, and as he came up over the ridge he saw a huge mountain range. Now why had he not seen that before? He walked along admiring the snowcapped peaks when he realized that he was walking in snow himself. "That I should have noticed," he said aloud. He grew nervous and decided that maybe Christian had the right idea. The straight and narrow path didn't look too bad right now. He turned, but his next step crunched through the snow and he found himself up to his waist. Two-Face became very aware of the fact that his feet were touching nothing. They dangled in the air below the surface of the snow.

He wondered if the drop beneath him was two feet or two hundred. He carefully placed one hand on either side of the hole he had created. He opened his palms out flat, because that is what it seemed like a person would do in this situation. As he moved to push himself up, the snow that was holding him in place gave way and he fell through the snow he had been walking on. The last thought in his head was, "Okay, two hundred. Now we know."

Halfway up the hill, the path Christian was on suddenly flattened itself out and Christian saw a park bench carved out of the rock. Someone who had traveled this way before, for some reason had come back and created this small resting spot for future travelers. Engraved on the bench were the words "Rest. It gets harder." Despite not having his book bag on him, Christian was very weary and he sat down to rest and listen to music and get his strength back. He rubbed the strange new tattoo with his thumb. It did not rub off and it did not hurt or itch. He was simply marked. Now and Forever.

He heard the shouts above the music in his ears and pulled the buds out and set them on the bench next to his iPod. He stood up as a man and a woman came running down the hill above him. The man stumbled once, but regained his footing. The two of them practically dropped into the small plateau where Christian was waiting.

The pair seemed to be a couple because they had matching Elvis T-shirts. They were identical, except the woman's said "Suspicious Minds" and the man's said "Surrender."

"What's going on?" Christian asked.

The couple were breathing heavy and the man had squatted down to keep from losing his balance. The woman said, "The farther you go the harder it gets."

"How hard can it be?" Christian said.

"Lions," the man breathed.

"What?" Christian said.

"Lions. Big Freaking Hairy Lions. Just sitting there by the path. We ran before they saw us. Nothing is worth this." Surrender held up his hand and Suspicious Minds took it and helped him to his feet. They began the slow walk back toward the narrow path.

Christian watched them go and then, steeling himself, he moved on. The path grew very steep and once or twice he found himself on all fours, practically crawling to the top of the hill. He had climbed a good hundred feet or more and knew that the evening was coming on. The idea of meeting lions at night was somehow scarier than meeting them in the daytime. He reached the top of the hill and looked back down the way he had come. Far below he saw the carved stone park bench. From here it was no bigger than his fingernail. But from where he stood he could still see his new iPod, sitting on the bench were he had left it.

He wanted to kick himself. For a moment he wondered if he could just keep going, but the shimmering one had said he was going to need it. There was nothing else to do. There was no other choice. He started back down the slope. He fell once and started to slide, but righted himself and managed to stay on his feet the rest of the way down. Standing on the plateau, he put the music device in his jacket pocket and turned. He was pretty sure the hill had gotten steeper. But he supposed that to be a trick of the light.

Chapter 8

Climbing in the dim light, it took what Christian thought was twice as long to get to the top of the same hill he had climbed just an hour before. When he reached the top of the steep slope for the second time, he saw a bright light in the distance. There, less than a mile or two away, Christian saw the bright light of a gigantic hotel. Bigger than any he had seen in any of the books he had read. Bigger than any that had been described to him by people who had left the City of Ruin and returned. There were giant flashing lights that illuminated the sky like Las Vegas. The sign read "The Palace."

He walked toward the hotel. Soon he was walking solely by the light of this grand, glorious building. The sun had gone down and even the moon was outshone by the dazzling lights of the Palace.

As he got closer Christian stopped and froze in his tracks. The two lions that Suspicious and Surrender had told him about were sitting on either side of the driveway that led up to the steps of the hotel.

"Stone," he thought. "They are stone lions, like outside of a library or some other building." They were much larger than average lions and in the light of the hotel they did look somewhat motionless. Christian wondered how the couple could have been so confused, but then he had seen so many other strange things on this trip that he supposed anything was possible. He took another step and one of the lions turned and looked at him. The growl that came from inside the beast was so low it made his stomach churn.

The doorman of the hotel saw Christian standing there and came out to the steps. He stood at the edge of the path just fifty yards away from where Christian was standing. "They are chained!" he called. "Trust me."

Christian peered at the lions, but he did not see any chains.

The doorman called again. "If you stay in the middle of the path, they cannot reach you. I promise."

One of the lions roared.

Christian was seized by an overwhelming desire to run back the way he had come. He supposed he could pass the Elvis couple and be back in his own bed in a matter of minutes.

Christian looked at the doorman, who was smiling at him from under his fine red cap. With his white gloves he motioned Christian to come forward.

Christian took a deep breath and walked toward the hotel. At the same instant, both lions jumped toward the path. Both were jerked back by chains at the last minute. Christian thought he was going to wet himself.

The lions roared. Being bigger than the average lion, the roar was bigger than the average roar. Christian could feel the breeze caused by the lions' roar. It smelled of foul meat and digested grain.

Keeping his eyes directly on the doorman, Christian walked straight ahead and actually hugged the doorman at the bottom of the steps. The doorman returned the hug and laughed.

"Who does your landscaping?" Christian said. "You might want to re-think the whole safari theme."

The doorman smiled and said, "Keeps the riff-raff out."

Christian nodded as if this made sense.

"And the lions fed," the doorman said, and turned away. "This way, sir."

Christian could not tell if the man was joking or not, but he followed anyway. They walked up the steps and the doorman grasped a large brass handle with both hands and pulled. The great wooden door swung open and the doorman said, "Welcome to the Palace."

Christian noticed an engraved gold name badge pinned to the Doorman's uniform. It said "Mr. Watchman." The doorman saw his gaze and said, "It is who I am and it is what I do."

Christian said, "What is this place?"

Mr. Watchman said, "It was built for weary travelers as a place to rest and recharge before moving on."

Christian liked the sound of the word rest.

"Have you eaten, sir?" the doorman asked.

"Uh...no," Christian said. It was the first time in his life he could remember anyone calling him sir.

Mr. Watchman led him over to the front desk. There was a large silver bell, the kind that doormen rang at one time. From behind a door a woman appeared. She was the most strikingly beautiful woman that Christian had ever seen. She smiled, not a hotel desk clerk smile, but a genuine, beautiful, you-are-so-welcome-here smile.

"May I help you?" she asked with a voice as soft as silk.

"I'm on my way to the City of Light," Christian said. "I've been on the road for days and I was hoping I could stay here for the night."

She asked, "You came through the gate?"

He nodded.

"Did you buy some jelly?" Christian felt in his pockets and came up with the remaining jar. He had eaten the biscuits and the cookies earlier.

The desk clerk smiled.

Christian cleared his throat. "I don't have any money. But I'd be willing to work if you had something you needed done."

The woman behind the counter said, "What have you got on you?"

Christian reached deep into the pockets of his coat and came up with the Magic 8 Ball the Preacher had given him. He laid it on the counter. He also had the candy bar from the rest stop, and of course the tattered book that had started him on the quest in the first place.

She said, "Is that all?" Christian could tell by the way she was looking at him that she already knew about the music device. He pulled it out of his pocket and laid it on the counter.

"I thought so," the woman said.

"I can't give you any of these things," Christian said. "I have a feeling I will need them on the rest of my journey and I don't have anything else, so I can do some job for you or I can sleep in your lobby or on the front step. Would it be all right if I did that?

Mr. Watchman chuckled and put his gloved hand over his mouth. Both Christian and the woman behind the counter looked at him. The doorman looked at the floor.

"This place is for people who are on a very special journey," she said. "You have these things, which means you were sent on that journey like others before you. The journey is hard enough. We don't charge for people who are on a pilgrimage."

Christian hadn't thought of his road trip as a pilgrimage.

"Have you eaten?" the woman asked.

"Not since this morning," Christian said.

She smiled and tapped the silver bell on her right. From behind the same door three girls appeared. They all seemed to be about Christian's age. They all smiled at him. They all looked a little like the woman who had welcomed him. "My daughters," the woman said.

"Hello," Christian said.

The three girls giggled. One had hair like her mother's. One had hair that seemed to have been dyed a bright red with a long black streak in the front. The other girl had long blonde hair that she had tied into a braid in the back. They all wore uniforms similar to their mother's.

"Our guest is tired and hungry," the Manager said. "Take him to his room. Keep him company. Let him rest until the chef has prepared something."

The girls practically ran around from the other side of the desk and took him by the hand and led him to the elevator.

"My name is Caren," the girl who seemed the oldest said, "only with a C and not a K."

"I'm Charity," said the one with red hair.

"I'm Goodness," said the one who seemed the youngest.

"Goodness?" Christian asked.

"When mother found out she was pregnant again, she said, "Oh my goodness." Goodness said this and smiled.

Charity said, "That's what not what she said, but she couldn't name you Holy Sh…"

"That's not true!" said Goodness angrily.

They stepped into the elevator. Caren pulled a plastic card from the pocket of her blue blazer. She slid it into the slot next to the top button on the panel. She pushed the button and a disembodied but pleasant voice said, "Penthouse Suite. Going Up."

Christian had only been in a hotel one time in his life. It had been a little out-of-the-way place with a smelly carpet and a moldy shower. The elevator he was riding in was actually nicer than the place he had stayed in before. "I could just sleep here," he thought.

The elevator stopped and the doors opened, not into a hallway, but into what was basically a lobby for the rest of the room. Marble pillars and marble floors led to five steps that led to a room with thick carpet and leather furniture. In front of him was a series of floor-to-ceiling windows that, at the moment, showed only the night sky. Christian could see a full kitchen, a dining room, and a pool table. There was a big-screen TV and an antique coke machine in the living room. It was the nicest room he had ever been in.

"Your bedroom is down that hall and on the left," Goodness said. "There's a hot tub in the bathroom or one out on the balcony if you'd prefer that one. Why don't you clean up and we'll get your clothes washed. Room service will be up in an hour or so. What would you like to eat?"

"I've never been in a place this nice," Christian said. He still had not moved from the spot where he stepped off the elevator.

The girls giggled. Caren took his hand and led him to a huge bedroom. The bed in the center of the room was bigger than his entire bedroom back home. Caren went to a cabinet and opened it. She pulled out towels the size of bed sheets. Hanging in the closet were white fluffy robes. She handed these to him.

Christian was looking out the window at the moon. Caren took his face in her hands and turned it to face hers. "You are one of God's pilgrims," she said. "You have been through much and you will be through more. You should enjoy this."

He started to speak but she stopped him. "Have a soak in the hot tub. Leave your clothes on the bed. Clean up. Feel better and then come out and we'll have room service and you can tell us the stories of what you've been through." She pulled his head down and kissed him gently on the forehead. She then spun him around and gave him a gentle shove toward the bathroom.

The bathroom was bigger than any Christian had ever seen.

An hour later Christian stepped out of the bathroom wearing the white fluffy robe Caren had given him. It wrapped around him and hung to the floor. He had relaxed in the hot tub and showered, with all manner of soaps and shampoos and conditioners. He had shaved and brushed his teeth and trimmed his nails and generally felt better than he had in a very long time.

He looked for his clothes but they weren't around. Cautiously he stepped out of the bedroom and was greeted by the smell of something wonderful.

The girls saw him and giggled. Their mother was there, too. She said, "We didn't know if you liked Chinese, Italian or a good old-fashioned burger and fries so we ordered some of everything." She motioned him over to the dining room table, which was covered with some of the most amazing food Christian had ever seen. They all walked to the table and Christian held out the chair for the girls' mother. It was something his father had taught him. "If it ever comes down to you and another guy..." his father had said, "the gentleman always gets the girl."

The other girls smiled and said "awwwwwwwwww." They sat down and whispered to each other. Christian sat down himself and inhaled the smell of the wondrous food.

"Thank you," Christian said. "Thank you for your hospitality."

"Tell us about your journey," Charity said.

For the next half hour Christian told them everything. The people he had met and the things he had seen and the shimmering beings that had given him the tattoo (which he also showed them). He told them of the bizarre things the woman with the floppy hat had shown him. He told them of the people and of Tux and Two-Face and which paths they had taken.

There was something about the look in the mother's eyes that told Christian that the two men had not reached—and never would reach—the other side of the hill.

"Can I ask you something?" Caren said.

"Sure." Christian squirted brown mustard on a pile of French fries. A waiter came out of the kitchen and set a large milkshake next to Christian. There was an Oreo cookie carefully broken and set afloat on top of the whipped cream.

"Do you ever think about home?"

Christian was quiet for a moment and then said, "Yeah, but they aren't usually good thoughts. I was going through the motions there. The motions of being a student, of being a friend, of being a son. I mean I miss my family, but I don't think I could have stayed and 'become' part of that. I don't think my family could have stood me. You know? I didn't like myself very much when I was there."

"Do you like yourself now?" The girls' mother asked. There was a bit of "mother" in her tone, but she was being sincere.

"I know that I feel very alive," Christian said. "I know that what I've been through has made me who I am and I haven't felt dead inside since I started."

She said, "There's a difference between feeling dead and not feeling alive."

Christian nodded. "I think I like myself better now," Christian said. "Is that what you mean?"

She smiled. "Sort of."

"I don't understand why they didn't come with you," Caren said.

"It's my journey," Christian said. "I can commit myself to this path, but I can't make someone else come with me. I can invite them. I can make the path a little better for them the way someone else made it better for me by marking the path or putting up that bench on the hill or making this nice place."

Charity said, "But shouldn't you be more forceful in getting others to come along or at least to take up the journey too?"

Christian thought and chewed a bit of Oreo that had come up in the straw. "You have been so good to me. I know you've been good to others on this path. That's what this place is for. I don't see why someone would hold it against you if you didn't follow the same path I did. There are so many people in the world. There must be more than one road to the City of Light."

He turned toward the mother of the three girls. "Don't you think so?"

She said, "I think it's time we let you get your rest. You have a big day tomorrow."

Christian swallowed. "I have a big day tomorrow?"

The girls giggled and their mother looked at him as if it was all she could do not to tuck him into bed and kiss him good night.

The mother and daughters stood up and said their good nights. They walked to the elevator. Christian started to clear the dishes, but a group of people emerged from the kitchen. An older woman took the dishes from his hand and said, "Now you just let me have those, you look dead-dog tired, you do. You go on to bed and I'll see you at breakfast."

Christian protested all the way to his bedroom, where she gave him a push and he walked over and lay down on the bed. He protested that he was perfectly capable of cleaning his own dishes and that he really wasn't tired, but in a moment he was deep in sleep.

*****

Christian did not remember a sleep like that one. Deep and dreamless and restful. Normally when he woke up it took him forever to get the energy to get out of bed. But this morning he felt energized and rested. He wandered out into the hallway and was met by the woman who had cleaned up after him the night before. She had a mug of coffee in her hand.

"Sunshine!" she said. She handed him the cup of coffee and pointed him toward the giant windows in the living room. There was a balcony that he had not seen the night before.

He slid the window aside and stepped out onto the balcony and felt the breeze blow through his hair. The sunshine felt good on his skin. "I could get used to this," he thought. Then realized that it was probably fear that was talking. Everyone seemed to be nice to him the way you would someone who was going to die. He began to gloom again, but then he sipped his coffee and watched the wind blow the trees. "I am a servant of the King," he said to himself. "I will go where I am sent."

He remembered a hymn from when he was a boy. And he sang it there on the balcony. He sang without embarrassment. Without worry about what it sounded like to others. He sang it for himself and for God.

Well I lift my eyes to heaven where the angels stand as one.
And I lift my eyes to heaven where the banquet has begun.
Singing glory to the father and the spirit and the son.
And I lift my eyes to heaven where the angels stand as one.
Well I lift my eyes to heaven for I know that belong.
And I lift my eyes to heaven and I join the angel throng.
They are gathered 'round the altar
*   and they sing a heavenly song.*
And I lift my voice to heaven and I know that I belong.

He sang until he ran out of the words he remembered and then re-sang the ones he did remember. He took the coffee back to his room and found that in the night someone had hung his clothes in his closet. Freshly washed! They felt comfortable. His jacket had been cleaned, but still held the worn look he loved about it.

As he came out of the room the woman who had given him the coffee (he was calling her Sunshine in his mind) was waiting in the hall. She refilled his mug and said, "They are waiting for you downstairs." For no reason that he could think of, Christian kissed her cheek and said, "Thank you."

He rode down the elevator sipping his coffee. When the doors opened the Manager, her daughters, and even Watchman the doorman were waiting for him.

Christian was overcome by a deep sense of loss. He nearly cried. These good people had taken him in without question, fed him, given him a place to sleep and treated him like he was royalty. Now just as suddenly it was time for him to leave.

The Manager stepped forward to meet him as he came into the lobby of the hotel. From behind her back she pulled out a canvas bag with a long strap. Across the front flap was sewn the word "Shalom," which means peace. "Take this with you," she said, looping it over his head. He raised his arm and put the bag to hang by his side. The strap lay across his chest, but it did not cut him like his book bag had done. Though the strap lay right on the scar on his right shoulder, it felt like it was healing him, not hurting him.

"You can carry all your things in it," she said. "I've already packed you some breakfast and lunch. It's big enough, there's lots of room, so you don't have to load up your pockets. Peace you will carry with you. You will feel it with you all the time."

Christian admired the bag and ran his hand over the stitching. "This is very nice," he said. Opening the bag he saw some food and fruit. At the bottom was a key. He removed and examined it carefully. It was a large key and engraved across the top was the word *Promise*.

Christian looked at the Manager. She said, "It will unlock many things."

Before Christian could ask what she meant, Caren came forward and hugged him. She kissed his cheek and said, "That's for luck."

Charity came and hugged him too. She kissed his other cheek and said, "That's for protection."

He released her as Goodness threw herself into his arms and kissed him full on the lips. Christian felt himself blush. She released him and said, "That's for me."

The other girls glared at their sister, but their mother simply smiled.

Christian started to say something and caught himself and finally said simply, "Thank you." There was such earnestness in his words that the Manager nearly cried.

"This way, sir," Watchman said, and he led Christian to the door. He opened it. Christian took a look back. All four women were waving. Christian smiled a hey-I'm-just-going-out-for-a-walk smile and went through the door.

When the door closed Watchman said, "Sir, if you don't mind, I have a gift for you as well."

Christian knew better than to say something stupid like "you shouldn't have" or "you didn't have to."

Watchman stepped over to a post and from behind it brought out a walking staff. It was easily six feet high and nearly perfectly straight, except of a slight twist in the middle. Around the top edge was a hand-painted pattern that Christian had never seen before. It had been stripped of bark and polished.

He handed it to Christian and the young man was immediately taken with its weight. "Heavy," he said.

"If I might say, sir," Watchman commented, "it's not just for walking."

Christian looked at him and Watchman made a swinging motion like a baseball batter.

"Ahhhhhhh," Christian said and wondered again exactly what he was going to be up against.

"God be with you," Watchman said, and extended his hand.

"And also with you." Christian took it.

"You be careful."

Christian nodded. Watchman walked Christian back down the path between the lions, who were still sleeping, to the straight and narrow path.

"Who was the last one to come this way?" Christian said. "I mean, before me."

"It was a girl," Watchman said. "Short black hair. Had a real fire in her. She came through two days ago."

Christian was surprised to hear it had been so recent. "Maybe I will catch up to her."

"Maybe," Watchman said.

Christian adjusted the canvas bag on his shoulder and tapped the staff on the ground twice and walked on.

Chapter 9

Christian was amazed how easy the walk was with the staff in his hand. "Why didn't I make one of these for myself a long time ago?" he wondered.

He allowed his thoughts to wander as he walked along. He thought of his family and the City of Ruin and of Plaz and Bull. They weren't so bad, were they? Had he been honest with the Manager and her daughters? Was the living at home really that bad? Christian stopped walking and refocused his mind on the path in front of him. He was worried. He knew that. Everyone at the Palace had treated him well, and yet he could not get the idea of the condemned man's last supper out of his mind. They had prepared him and were praying for him because of what he was *about* to face, not for what he *had* faced. Whatever he was going to meet along the way from here on out would be worse than anything so far. He walked a little quicker. "There will be many challenges," Christian said aloud to himself, trying to sound deep and theological. But it did little to ease his mind. "There will be many things that scare the crap out of you," he said. This too did little to ease his mind, but at least he felt he was being honest with himself.

Over the next ridge Christian saw his first "challenge."

The man was standing by the path. He was very tall and bigger in the shoulders than Watchman the doorman. He wore a suit that Christian assumed was an Armani, though he had honestly never seen an Armani suit before. The man stood by the path with his hands folded in front of him. A gold ring was wrapped around each finger. His hair was long and soft-looking and hung past his shoulders. "Good morning, Christian," the man said.

His voice had a thick accent that Christian could not place. Christian thought, "Here's a guy with pretty hair, lots of rings, a suit that costs more money than my father made in a year and he already knows my name as I'm walking along the path that will be filled with things to scare the crap outta me. Yep, it's a good day."

Christian walked past the man with his extended hand and didn't look at him. He heard a slight chuckle behind him.

Christian crested the next ridge and saw the man waiting for him again. Standing beside the path, smiling this time. Christian was going to turn around, but he knew that the man wasn't there, so he moved forward, a little more cautiously this time.

The man spoke again. "Most people would at least exchange a greeting with someone who greets them."

"Most people," Christian said.

"You don't remember me, do you?" the man in the Armani suit asked. He walked along beside the path keeping pace with Christian.

"Should I?"

"We met once before, only briefly. My name is Lyon." (He pronounced it Lee-Oh-n)

"Doesn't ring a bell." Christian kept moving and did not look at him. In his head, Christian thought, "Oh them Lyons they can eat my body..."

"We met the night of Plaz's twelfth birthday party, when you and all your friends played with the Ouija board."

Christian stopped in his tracks. Lyon smiled. Christian thought he had too many teeth for a human.

"Ha!" said Lyon. "Now you remember."

"It was a kids' game," Christian said. "Plaz was moving the little gizmo, anyway. He told me he was."

"He was scared," Lyon said. "He convinced himself that he had moved it."

Christian noticed that no matter where he walked or stopped on the path, Lyon did not put a foot on it.

"You said," Lyon continued, "if there *are* demons, show yourself and make your presence known to us and I will serve thee." Lyon threw his arms in the air (just as Christian had done at the party) and he also spoke with Christian's twelve-year-old voice (complete with the I'm-going-through-an-embarrassing-puberty cracking.)

"I was twelve," Christian said. "I was kidding around."

Christian had stopped walking. Lyon lightly sidestepped, causing Christian to turn in order to face him. He didn't want Lyon behind him.

"Yes," Lyon said. "True. However, once you make a promise it would be very un—shall we say—Christian to break it."

"I'm serving a different Master now," Christian said.

"Ah yes..." Lyon said again. "A Master who has put you in danger how many times since you left your home?"

Christian turned and walked on. Behind him Lyon called, "You never did say good-bye to your family, did you?"

Christian turned and Lyon was gone. He cursed himself for being suckered like that. He crested the next ridge knowing Lyon would be there.

He was.

When he got closer Lyon said, "Everybody thinks you ran away from home to join the circus. You mother cries every night. Your father makes up lies to tell people that you call all the time. Your sister, well she tried to defend you to a bully at school. She punched his lights out and then got expelled for fighting."

Christian slowed his pace, but he was not aware of it.

"You're actually more trouble since you left," Lyon said.

Christian kept walking.

"You've pretty much disappointed everyone around you, haven't you? Your family, your friends. The Preacher gives you a simple instruction and you couldn't even do that right."

Christian's grip tightened on the walking staff. He walked faster, leaving Lyon behind him, but knowing he'd be waiting on the other side of the next ridge. And he was.

"Your greatest fear is to be like them. Isn't it?" Lyon said. "You left, more than anything else, so you wouldn't turn out like your family. Selfish reason."

Christian tried to ignore him.

"You don't have to go to the City of Light to change things," Lyon said. "You could have fixed things right there. How is running away going to solve any problem in that community? You could be more socially aware. You could run for school board and change the school. Then for City Council and change the way the city operates. Then you could run for mayor and change everything, even the name of the city. You'd be on CNN as the youngest mayor in the country, who actually made a difference. Did it ever occur to you that you were supposed to make a City of Light right where you were?"

Christian stopped and turned on Lyon and went to poke him in the chest with his finger. "Look, you…"

But that was all Lyon needed. He grabbed Christian's hand and yanked him off the path. Christian tripped and fell hard, losing his walking staff and rolling ten or fifteen feet off the path.

Lyon brushed the hair out of his face and said, "Whoa, that felt good to do that."

He walked toward Christian, who was struggling to get to his feet, and grabbed him by the front of his jacket and threw him again. Christian landed with a thud and rolled, purposely this time, thinking he could get to his feet before Lyon was on him again. He stood up and saw that Lyon had somehow grabbed the canvas bag that the Manager had given him. He was rummaging through it like an animal. "*Cookies!*" Lyon said and began to rip open the paper bag the Manager had put the cookies in.

Christian looked at the walking staff that was lying just a few feet off the path.

"Uh can git toof fit beefur you kinnn!" Lyon said, with his mouth full of cookies.

Christian made a break for the staff. Lyon dropped the bag and ran for it at the same time. In the last instant Christian pivoted and ran toward Lyon, head-butting him in the stomach. Lyon sprayed cookie crumbs from his mouth like an aerosol can and fell backward. Christian spun again and got to the staff and picked it up.

In that brief moment Christian was pretty sure he saw Lyon for what he really was and it was all he could do not to scream. Lyon was charging at him. Christian chocked up on the staff like a baseball bat and swung the way Watchman had shown him. He connected with Lyon's head.

Lyon went down to the ground. Hitting the grass, he immediately looked like the long-haired man in the Armani again. Christian backed himself up on the path again and stood with the staff on his shoulder ready to swing again. Lyon turned and looked at him. Half of his skull was gone and he was bleeding profusely. Except he wasn't bleeding blood. From the wound poured thousands of tiny insects, locusts no bigger than a match head. They "dripped" onto his suit and into and out of his mouth. Lyon started to laugh.

Christian tightened up on the staff and swung again. This time the bat whiffed though the air. He hadn't missed. Lyon was gone.

Christian spun around twice looking for him, but he had completely vanished again. Christian ran to the top of the ridge, but Lyon was not waiting on the other side as he had been before. He was simply gone. Christian walked down the ridge and, using the staff as a sort of fishing pole, was able to loop the strap of the canvas bag with all his belongings. The paper sack with the remaining cookies was on the grass, but Christian decided he had lost his taste for cookies.

He straightened the canvas bag on his shoulder and continued on. He walked for another two or three hours trying to shake the image from his mind of that one brief moment when Lyon hadn't been a long-haired man in an Armani. He actually shook his head several times trying to clear the image, thinking maybe it would be like shaking the Etch-A-Sketch he had when he was a kid. No luck. He thought of other things, specifically the kiss that Goodness had given him. That helped a lot. Later he would decide that seeing Lyon the way he did would be like a scar on his brain. It would never fully heal but it might fade over time. That helped a little too.

The path he was on sloped downward and Christian saw smoke up ahead. As it got closer he noted that there was no smell of smoke. It was just dark. As if the sun itself were not allowed to shine in this particular spot. Closer still he saw that the path ahead sloped down into a valley and there were no paths around it.

In the center of the path was a huge white building, its bricks standing out clean and bright in the darkness. The entryway of glass and metal stood five stories tall. Christian could hear a soothing orchestral version of the Beatles' *With a Little Help from My Friends* pumped through the scratchy outdoor speakers.

The straight and narrow path, the one the Preacher had told him not to leave, the one that the scary demon in the Armani suit had pulled him off of in order to attack...that path led straight into quadruple entry doors.

Brass letters hung above the entry in an arch that gleamed in the un-natural darkness. The letters spelled out "Valley of the Shadow of Death Mall."

"Well, that's subtle," Christian said to no one in particular.

As he stepped through the doors into the fluorescent-lit atrium, Christian immediately noticed the complete absence of the "straight and narrow path."

"First thing to do is find the exit," Christian thought.

He wandered in and found himself in what—in any normal mall—would have been a food court. But the smells that came from the fast-food shops were rancid-smelling. The first person he encountered was a guy about his age who appeared to have taken the personal hygiene rules in the employees' handbook as optional. The smell he gave off was overpowering and the grease in his hair literally dripped onto the tray he was holding, as he offered free samples to passersby. He held the tray out to Christian, who backed away from it when he saw that whatever the free sample was...it apparently had fingernails.

People of different nationalities, ages, genders all wandered the halls without looking at each other or at him. Christian decided they weren't really "looking" at all. They were simply wandering. Glazed-over mindless meandering.

Christian saw an old man carrying a bag similar to the one he had over his own shoulder. Christian wondered if the old man had been to the Palace and had been given a bag by the Manager. He wondered if the old man had been a young man when he got there and was now going to live out his days in a mind-numbing haze. As Christian looked for an exit, he passed shops on either side of him. The mannequins that stood in the window looked too lifelike to be plastic. Some of them blinked. Some of them shifted from foot to foot, but they did not leave the display window. Christian thought these were people who, after growing too indifferent to even wander the mall, simply stopped moving altogether.

"If they just decided to stop moving," Christian thought, "then someone had to prop them up in the window and dress them in the clothes." His next thought was about the Valley of the Shadow of Death Mall's employees and the kind of people who would work there.

He didn't wonder long. A moment later Christian heard the squeak of a cart and the happy whistle of someone pushing it. Ahead of him, coming toward him down the aisle was an "employee" of VSDM. The man was older than his father but easily twice the size. He was twelve feet tall with shoulders the size of a bus. His skin was a deep red, as if the blood on the inside was pushing so hard to get out, that if you just bumped him he'd pop like a balloon. Christian turned his eyes forward and tried not to make eye contact. He remembered that he could glaze his eyes over whenever his father lectured him. (This was something that infuriated his father and Christian knew it. He felt a sudden pang of remorse for treating his father that way, but he pushed the thought aside.) The "employee" wore a bright blue shirt with the word "Neville" stitched over the breast pocket. "I will fear Neville," Christian thought to himself. He watched as Neville stopped his cart near a bench where two middle-aged women with perfect housewife haircuts were sitting. They looked (and apparently smelled, judging from Neville's expression) like they had been sitting there for a very long time. Both looked up at Neville with hazy indifference. Neville picked each one up and dropped them into the trash can on the front of his cart. The can appeared to be no bigger than the trash cans at Christian's school, but he could see that the women's bodies seemed to plummet down inside and disappear completely.

Trying to look in front of him and NOT at Neville on his way by, the two passed each other. Christian could feel Neville's gaze on the back of his head. He did not turn around. He kept walking. He suddenly found himself humming the Muzak tune that was piping from the speakers overhead and quite literally bonked himself in the head with the staff to make himself quit. "I have to get out," he thought. "I have to find an exit now or I'm going to eventually wind up in the window of a very old Old Navy."

From behind him Christian heard what he was sure was Neville's voice. It shouted, "We got a live one here!" This was followed by the sound of running feet. Christian turned around to see Neville the giant running toward him and shoving wandering shoppers out of the way. Christian ran. He didn't have a direction in mind. He simply knew that "away" was the best direction at the moment. He ran down the hall, slaloming between and around pasty-faced zombies. Neville's feet seemed to have been joined by several others. Other sounds told Christian that his pursuers were not actually taking the time to dodge people. They were simply tossing them out of the way. He heard a window crash, and the thought in his mind of what made it was graphic enough to make him not turn around to see if he was right.

Christian skidded around a turn and ran to his left. More zombie-eyed shoppers. More footsteps behind him. He grabbed a garbage can as he passed it and pushed it over. (He had seen this in a cop-buddy movie. It hadn't worked then either.)

"STOP. Security. STOP. Security." Someone behind him shouted in a voice that didn't sound fully human. Ironically it was not the first time he'd heard it. He remembered a time when he and Plaz had decided to see if you could actually stay for twenty-four hours in a twenty-four-hour S-Mart. (For the record, the answer is 9 hours and 45 minutes.)

Christian jumped over a bench and made a left down another hallway. Suddenly he heard a girl's voice shout *"Here! Over here!"*

From the corner of his eye he saw a light. It was a doorway that opened into daylight. With no idea where he was going and no other options open to him, Christian ran toward the light. A girl was standing at the exit holding the door open just enough for someone to run through. Christian ran toward her. She opened it just a little more and Christian jumped and turned his body sideways. He landed on his feet on the pavement outside and turned around. She was pushing the door closed and Christian pushed with her. Neville and the others who had been chasing him slammed against the glass.

Christian looked into Neville's eyes as he pushed up close to the glass and slowly raised the walking staff Christian had dropped just before sliding through the door. Neville began to lick the staff with a thick green tongue. "Aw no," Christian said.

"Oh, gross!" the girl said. The other "security" or "maintenance" people backed off of Neville and stood looking at the two people on the other side of the door. Neville smiled, but it was one of those smiles you see on a bully who knows he's been caught smoking, but doesn't want the teacher to know it bothered him. All of them backed up without turning.

Christian looked at the girl who had saved his skin and said, "They can't leave."

She said, "Not till quitting time?"

Christian sat down hard on the sidewalk breathing heavy. "Thanks," he said. "You saved my skin."

She looked at him sitting there and said, "I think that's what they serve in the food court."

Christian's stomach turned. She held out a hand to help him to his feet. He took it Neville and his companions still had not stopped looking at the two of them.

"My name is Christian," Christian said, still trying to catch his breath.

"I'm Faith," she said.

"Well, that's ironic," he said.

"Don't you think?" she said, and he looked at her as if to say "I don't believe you just said that."

She said, "City of Light?"

He put his hands on his knees and nodded.

She smiled and said, "You want a traveling companion?"

Chapter 10

Christian finally stood up and got a good look at the girl who had rescued him. She was tall. Her straight black hair was cut roughly, as if she had done it herself without the benefit of a mirror. Black wristbands, black jeans, and a black T-shirt that read "Jesus called. He wants his religion back" in bright pink letters.

"That was a nice staff," she said. "Pity it got all slimmed." He smiled.

"Was a gift," Christian said. "Did you come by way of the Palace?"

"Weren't those people a trip?" she said. "I see you got a bag, too."

He straightened it on his shoulder. She showed him hers. The same African-type print that was on his walking staff was on her bag. His had been a plain canvas.

"They must have like a gift shop or something," she said.

"Did you come by way of the gate?" he asked.

"Uh-huh. You?"

He nodded.

"Look," she said. "You want to walk together awhile? We can see how far we get and you can tell me your story and I can tell you mine."

Christian took a deep breath. "Yeah. "S'go."

And the two walked together.

"So you stayed with Will Goodman?" Christian asked as they walked.

"Yeah," she said. "Nice old guy. I liked him. You met the woman with the floppy hat?"

He laughed and nodded.

"She was a stitch! Where did she send you?"

"Toward the hill with the cross," said Christian.

"I didn't get to a hill," she said. "Lady sent me through this small town that had a huge cross in the center of town."

The two stopped and looked at each other. "There's more than one path?" she asked.

"Not more than one path," Christian said. "Maybe it's just more than one journey?"

They both thought for a moment as they walked. Christian said, "Can I ask you something."

"That's why we're together."

"I had a backpack. Been carrying it forever. Preacher called it my baggage. Soon as I touched the cross on the hill it fell off and dropped into a deep hole. Did you have something like that?"

"Sort of," she said. "I had been branded."

"You mean like in…" he started.

"Yeah," she said. "Only I did it to myself. Burned me every day of my life as far back as I can remember. Like a big scarlet letter 'L.' I got to this little town with the cross in the middle and as soon as I touched it, the brand went away."

"Did you meet the angels?"

"Three guys in shiny clothes? Yeah. I met them. Was one of them that took my brand away by touching it. The other gave me an iPod."

Christian reached into his bag and pulled out his device.

She smiled. "Cool. Mine's black."

"What happened after the small town?

Her mood got dark and she said, "I almost didn't leave. I met this guy, really dad-ish. He had this used vinyl store. Man, it was a sweet setup! I spent the day hanging out in the store and he had this smokin' hot daughter. Her and me…"

Faith turned toward Christian and looked at him. "Is this going to be a problem? Cuz if it is we're done right here. I spent too long being told…"

"It's not a problem," Christian said.

She said, "He had this daughter and she and I got on really well. I was really thinking I could fall for her and then her dad offers me a job in the store. Says I can work there forever. Live in his house. He'd take care of me, ya know?"

Christian nodded.

"So I'm just about to accept the offer. Chuck all this pilgrimage stuff. She gives me a kiss and a hug and tells me in my ear that the guy's a letch and not really her father and that I should keep going."

"You didn't try to get her out of there?"

"I tried like hell!" Faith said loudly. "I even tried to tell her that we could sneak her out in the middle of the night, but she wouldn't go. She wouldn't leave the guy. What makes a girl do that? Why wouldn't she just run?"

"Fear," Christian said. "When the fear of the unknown is stronger that the fear of the known...a person will put up with almost anything."

Faith was quiet for a long time. Then she said, "You saw the lions?"

"Oh geez," he said. "Thought I was going to lose it."

"Me too. Watchman come out and call to you?"

He nodded. "Strange. Same journeys but different paths."

"Okay," she said, "Let me ask you one. You left the Palace, what did you run into?"

Christian had a sudden flash in his mind of Lyon and his 'true form.' "Guy with long girl's hair, lots of rings, and a nasty left hook."

"But—" she said, "what was he really?"

Christian thought. "I guess he was guilt or self-centeredness? I'm not sure. Made me feel like crap for leaving my family. Tried to make me turn around and pulled the 'change the world from your own backyard' thing. You?"

"Was a woman," she said. "Looked a lot like this old teacher of mine. Tried to make me ashamed of who I am because of the way I am." She looked at him cautiously again. He nodded.

"Funny thing is, she was one too. Back in school everybody knew you didn't go to her room for after-school tutoring. She used to just verbally abuse girls in class. Don't know why she'd show up here."

Neither said anything for awhile. Finally Christian said, "Like the shirt."

"Thanks," she said. "I like your shoes."

And then things were normal between them. They were just two friends on a hike. They talked about school and parents and God and how the Preacher had come to meet them the first time. It was as though they each finally had someone who understood and would listen because they had been there too.

After awhile Faith said, "This is going to get worse, isn't it?"

Christian tried to be reassuring. "Maybe not."

"No," she said. "Everybody has warned us along the way. I really don't think we've seen the worst yet."

Christian was quiet. He didn't want to say so, but he was thinking the same thing.

Chapter 11

Christian and Faith continued on together talking as two people who had known each other for years, discovering things about themselves as they discovered things about each other.

At one point toward noon they passed an abandoned gas station along the road. There was a "CLOSED" sign that hung from what was left of the door. Dim lights flickered inside, but the place was abandoned.

"Empty," Christian said, "but it's got power. You think the Pepsi machine still works?"

"Can't hurt to look. They stepped off the road and walked over to the service station. The gas pumps had been removed and metal caps had been welded onto the pipes. "They wouldn't leave gas in the tanks underneath?" she said.

"Seems like they'd empty them. Probably put the caps on too for safety. Kids come along and try to see the bottom of the tank by lighting a match."

"Damn teenagers," Faith said. Christian laughed.

Just inside the door was a soda machine. The word "antique" was not old enough to describe it. Christian put his hand against it. "Still running," he said.

On the left side of the machine was a long narrow glass door.

Faith opened it and slipped her hand inside. "Feels cool. You have any change?"

Christian fished around in his pockets and came up with some quarters. He bought two bottles and the pair used the opener on the side of the machine. They stood there a moment in the dark service station enjoying the shade. "Should we get two more for the road?" he asked.

"Only if you're going to carry this machine the whole way so we can use the opener.

"We could pry the opener off and take it with us.

Faith said, "We could pry open the machine and take all the soda too. But do you really want to push the ethics of stealing on this trip?"

"Point taken," Christian said. "But I'll buy another round and we can drink them as we walk."

"Sold."

From outside they heard a "Helllooooooooooooooooooo?"

Christian and Faith looked at each other. Faith held a finger to her lips. They waited.

"Is someone there?"

Stepping into the filling station was a tall man, about forty. His hair was cut in a perfectly trimmed 50's hairstyle. As if he had just got out of the military three months ago. He wore glasses and a polo shirt with a Faith Creek River Church logo embroidered over the left breast pocket. He had a Bible in his hand. It looked new. The three looked at each other a moment. "Oh, hello," the tall man said. "Anyone else going to the City of Light?"

"Sorry," Faith said. "You can't be too careful on this road."

"Absolutely," the tall man said. As he stepped into the light of the humming soda machine Christian suddenly recognized him. His eyes opened and he very nearly said something, but instead took a step back so his face was in the shadows.

He said, "Well, my name is Chad Converse. People call me Chatter."

"Faith," Faith said, extending her hand.

"Faith," Chatter repeated as he shook it.

"This is Christian," Faith said.

Christian leaned out just far enough to extend his hand.

"Christian," Chatter said, as if he had learned that the best way to memorize names was to repeat them on introduction.

"Does this thing work?" Chatter asked.

"Seems to. Even still cold," Faith said.

"Wonderful." Chatter reached into the pocket of his khaki pants and came up with a quarter. "Can I buy anyone else a round, so to speak? Heh heh."

"We're good," Christian said. Faith looked at him questioningly. "You'll excuse me, I'm going to see if the restroom is still working."

Faith could see his eyes in the dim light. "I'll go along," she said. "We'll be right back."

Chatter had pulled a bottle of soda out of the machine, opened it and was sipping it slowly. "Oh take your time. I'm looking forward to having someone to talk to. I mean, the Lord and I chat all the time." He said this waving his Bible. "But it will be nice to hear an *audible* voice."

Christian disappeared around the corner and Faith followed him. "What gives?" she whispered.

"We need to cut this guy loose, now," Christian said.

"Why?"

"He was my old Sunday School teacher when I was in junior high school. This guy is more than a little scary. I think we should find a way to let him go on without us."

She looked at him, surprised. "You hypocrite."

He looked shocked.

"You're on this path and so is he. Obviously someone sent him like they sent us. After all your talk about different journeys you're just going to cut this guy loose? He seems a little smarmy but there may be strength in numbers down the road."

"Trust me," Christian said, "you won't want to have this guy around much."

"I can handle him," she said. With that, she left Christian standing there. He actually did have to use the restroom. The door was unlocked but the light didn't work, so he propped it open wide enough to provide him some light to do what he needed to do. The sink worked too.

Coming back around the corner Christian saw Faith and Chatter talking. Chatter was smiling. When he looked up he said, "We know each other, don't we?"

Christian smiled. "Uh-huh. I was in your Sunday school class when I was in junior high."

"I remember you." Chatter's face smiled. But his eyes didn't .

"Are you traveling alone?" Faith asked.

"We're never really alone, are we?" Chatter said, and waved the Bible in his hand again.

"I guess you're right." Faith smiled. Christian could see it was already becoming the kind of smile you put on at the family reunion when everyone pretends that they forgot what everyone said last year. "So, is your name like the shoe?"

It was a silly question but one that she thought would start them out right. Chatter chuckled. He'd heard it before. "No. But I wish I had some of his money. Heh heh."

Christian was walking four or five feet behind them.

"So, Christian, we haven't seen you in church for a long time."

Christian said, "Yeah, I know. Hard to get there sometimes."

Chatter gave his Bible a little wave. "Youth Group meetings are really great. This year they may go to Mexico for a mission trip depending on how well the fundraiser goes."

Faith said, "You talk like this is a round-trip deal for you."

"Well, sure," Chatter said. "I just want to find the City of Light and then go back and encourage people to follow my example."

Faith looked behind them at Christian who made a "toldya" face.

"It's sort of a calling thing, isn't it?" Faith asked. "I thought it was more of an 'answering the call' journey rather than like a convention."

"That's one way of looking at it," Chatter said. "I'm going so I can renew myself and take that back and share it with others." He looked over at Faith and said, "If you don't mind my asking—are you going to change your shirt before you get there?"

"I thought it was funny," Faith said.

"It's making fun of Jesus," Chatter said. "You think he'll appreciate it? You might want to cut back on the eye shadow as well."

Behind them Christian snorted.

"And you know what Jesus would appreciate and what he wouldn't?"

Chatter turned at her and waved his Bible in the air again. He said, "I know my Bible, young lady. Tell her, Christian."

"He knows his Bible, young lady," Christian said.

Chatter turned and looked at Christian over his shoulder. "See, it's that kind of attitude that got you in trouble with Mrs. Coldiron."

"Mrs. Coldiron?" Faith said.

"Sounds like a party just waiting to happen, doesn't it?" Christian said.

"Mrs. Coldiron taught Christian in Sunday School," Chatter said. "Poor woman had to retire after 50 years of teaching. Said he had just taken all the fun out of it." He looked over his shoulder again. "That was why we told your parents not to bring you back anymore."

Faith said, "But you just told him how much you missed him."

"We miss all of the lost sheep, young lady. Jesus rejoices when they are found again."

"Ah," Faith said. "And once you find a lost sheep, what then?"

"Well, we hope they'll turn away from their sinful lives and be one of God's chosen."

"And you have to turn away to be one of God's chosen."

"It's all right here." He waved the book at her again.

Faith turned back toward Christian, who was grinning at her. She mouthed the words "If he waves that book at me again I'm going to take it from him."

Christian snorted again.

"So, Mr. Converse," Faith started.

"Call me Chatter," he said smiling. Faith wondered if he knew he was walking faster.

"Chatter," she said. "If Christian is on his way to the City of Light wouldn't you think that God 'chose' him?"

"God calls all sorts of people."

"Even ones with Jesus T-shirts and too much eye shadow," Christian said from behind them.

Chatter rolled his eyes dramatically.

"Yes, what part of the scripture does that come from exactly?" Faith asked.

"Second Kings," Chatter said. "Jezebel, the prostitute, painted her eyes and arranged her hair to mock the men who love the Lord."

"Are you calling me a whore?" Faith asked.

"I'm saying you paint your eyes like one to look alluring. That's all I'm saying to you."

Faith touched his arm and said, "Do I look alluring to you?" She batted her eyes at him.

"Jezebel mocked the good Christian men and she was fed to the dogs," Chatter said.

"I assure you," Faith said. "I have no intention of alluring men."

"Be that as it may," Chatter said. "Second Corinthians and the book of Philippians both say we should approach God with fear and trembling. That T-shirt mocks Jesus and just because…. wait a minute, what did you just say?"

Christian bowed his head and tried not to laugh.

"What?" Faith asked.

"You just said you had no intention of alluring men."

"Yes, I did say that."

"Well, then what…I mean why wou….You're not one of *those*, are you?"

"One of what?" she asked.

"I mean," Chatter sputtered, "you're not, you know, a gay. Are you?"

"You mean a lesbian?" she asked.

Christian said, "Wasn't Jamie Farr on MASH a lesbian?"

They both stopped and looked at him.

"Oh wait," Christian said, "that's Lebanese."

Faith looked at him. "Don't help me."

"'Kay."

"Would that be a problem if I was a lesbian?"

"You can't be," Chatter said. "You're a very pretty young girl."

"Pretty girls can't be lesbians?"

Christian said, "Clearly you don't go to the right websites."

"Don't help me," Faith said.

"I just mean...." Chatter said.

"What?" Faith asked. "That I'm not allowed on the road trip to the City of Light if I like girls?"

"The Bible says..." Chatter started flipping the pages.

"Heeeeeeeeere we go," Christian said.

"You're not going to trot out the abomination verses are you?" Faith asked.

"The book of Leviticus clearly states that for someone to..."

"Leviticus is referring to temple prostitution," Faith said. "Idol worship. It also says don't eat shellfish. And Leviticus 19:19 says don't wear two different kinds of materials woven together. What's your shirt made out of?"

"That's not the same thing!" Chatter said. He was flipping through the pages frantically.

"Romans 1:26?" she asked

Chad "Chatter" Converse stopped and looked at her.

"Yeah, I know that one," she said. "But look at the verses that come before verse 26. Paul was talking about people who worship in their church by having sex with everything that moves. In other words, a Roman orgy. Not two people who fall in love and want to spend the rest of their lives together and *happen* to be of the same gender."

Chatter started flipping again.

"She's got an answer for all of them," Christian said behind him.

"You're right," Chatter said. "We can love the sinner but hate the sin."

Christian said, "I thought Jesus said love the sinner but hate your own sin."

Chatter said, "Who am I to judge? But once we get to the City you'll have to renounce your ways in order to get through the gate."

He waved the Bible at Faith again and in an instant she had snatched it out of his hand and smacked him on the head with it. "Now," she said, "let's look up what God hates, shall we?"

"Give me that!" Chatter said, holding his head where she had belted him.

"No no no!" she said. "Let's look up what God hates. God hates fags, right? Isn't that what it says on the signs in the parking lots? God hates fags, so let's look that up. Proverbs 6:16.... Here it is.... Proverbs 6:16-19. 'There are six things the Lord hates, seven that are detestable to him: haughty eyes, a lying tongue, hands that shed innocent blood, a heart that devises wicked schemes, feet that are quick to rush into evil, a false witness who pours out lies and a man who stirs up dissension among brothers.'"

"Hey, wait a minute!" she said. "What happened to 'fags'? I swear 'fags' was in here! I mean would the guy with the sign on the street corner lie?"

Chad grabbed the Bible back from her. "You just won't listen, will you? Your type never does."

"What's my type?" Faith said. "Pretty little lesbians who paint their eyes?"

He looked at Christian. Christian shrugged. "So, what time is youth group on Sunday? We don't want to be late."

They had come to a place in the road where the path split into two different directions. This time there was no path up the center. It was clearly a choice. One way or the other.

Chatter Converse looked pale. "Which direction are you going?"

"Which direction are *you* going?" Faith asked. She batted her eyes at him and Chatter Converse turned red. "I think it would be better if we didn't travel together," Chatter said.

"You're getting that feeling, are you?" Faith asked.

"We're going left," Christian said. He was eager to be done with this conversation and keep moving.

"Fine, then," Chatter said. "I'll go right and I want you both to know"—he paused here and started to wave the Bible again; then thought better of it and put it behind his back—"that I will be praying for both of you."

"That's very kind," Christian said. "Very...uh...Christian of you."

Chapter 12

A few miles down the road, Faith was still laughing about the conversation with Chatter Converse. "I thought he was going to cry. That was just so cool."

"It wasn't cool," said Christian. "It was bizarre."

"You're just jealous because you blew the exit line."

"I didn't blow the exit line."

"Very Christian of you?" Faith laughed. "That's the best you could come up with?"

"What he doesn't get," Christian said, "is that everybody gets the grace of God. I mean he *says* everybody gets the grace of God but what he means is that everybody who thinks like he does gets the grace of God."

"Yeah? So?" Faith said.

"So yeah, he's going to be real surprised when they have a big party in the City of Light and you and I are both there."

"I can't wait to see the look on his face," Faith said. "I'm not getting what your problem is."

"My problem is that *he* will be there. This guy who is full of his own righteousness is going to be there too, and that ticks me off! Which makes me no better than him."

"You are so much better than him," Faith said.

"No. I'm not," Christian said. "At least, I'm not supposed to be. That guy really ticked me off, and now I'm wondering why I was told to go on this road trip in the first place."

They walked quietly for a moment and finally Faith said, "You're on this road trip because you are a good person. The Preacher saw that. He didn't send you because you were perfect. You're not here because you think you're right. You're here because you want to learn. You heard Chatter. He didn't even meet the Preacher. He came in through some shortcut and thought that Jesus is just going to confirm everything he already thinks is true. I'd say there's a difference."

"Doesn't feel like it right now," Christian said.

"Look," she said, grabbing his shoulder and spinning him around to face her. "If we get to the City of Light and the door is closing, would you hold it open for me?"

"Sure," he said, as if it were not a question.

"Would you hold it open for him? I mean, when it comes right down to it, would you hold it open for him too?"

"I guess I would," Christian said.

"You think he would do the same for us?"

"I'm really not sure," Christian said.

"Well, then that's where it has to stand for the moment, doesn't it?"

They continued to debate the merits of who was "getting in" into the afternoon, when they spotted a lemonade stand on the side of the road.

"Thirsty?" Christian asked.

Faith said, "Yeah, but you don't really think this is just your junior-wants-to-be-the-next-Trump, do you?"

As they got closer to the lemonade stand the figure behind the bench pushed back his broad brimmed hat and Christian and Faith saw it was the Preacher. His sparkling eyes peeked out from behind his dark glasses.

"Lemonade?" he asked.

"Preacher!" Faith shouted. She leaned over the counter of the stand and hugged him, knocking off his hat. She picked it up and put a kiss on his bald head, then put the hat back in place.

"Good to see you!" Christian said, and the two shook hands heartily.

"How's the journey been?" Preacher asked. He handed each of them a tall freezing glass of lemonade.

"Weird," Christian said, and proceeded to tell him about the adventure in the mall.

"Is that where you two met up?" Preacher asked.

"Saved his white ass," Faith said.

"My ass didn't need saving," Christian said.

"Yeah, right," Faith laughed.

They told the Preacher about Chatter Converse and of stopping by the home of the woman with the floppy hat. Christian wanted to ask the Preacher about what Chatter had told them, but down deep he seemed to be afraid of what the answer might be.

Faith drained the bottom of her glass and the ice slid forward and bumped her nose. She wiped her mouth and nose with her hand. "Whoops!" she said. The Preacher chuckled.

"What are you doing here?" Christian said. "Are we almost done or something?"

"Very nearly," the Preacher said, "but you have much more to see and pass through."

Neither of the travelers liked the look on the Preacher's face. "Is it going to get worse?" Faith asked.

"It could," Preacher said.

"We should have taken the other road," Faith said.

Preacher smiled. "Not necessarily. You chose this way. This one goes this way."

"Where is this way?"

The Preacher sighed. He didn't smile when he spoke. "You're going to pass through a small city. There will be no daylight. Only night. You will see a whole lot of people who gave up."

"What do you mean, 'gave up'?" Christian asked.

"You'll see," the Preacher said. "It's not going to be easy. They won't understand why you do what you do. And they probably won't let you go your own way like Mr. Converse did. This will be different."

Nearby the lemonade stand was a tall tree. Christian and Faith sat down and rested and thought quietly about all they had been through. The Preacher quietly gathered the glasses and the cooler and tucked his chair under his arm. "I need to go."

Christian and Faith stood up. Christian said, "Will we see you again?"

The Preacher just looked over his shoulder and smiled as he walked back down the path in the direction that Christian and Faith had come.

Christian looked up. "Gonna be dark soon."

"Best time to go into a city where there is no day," she said. "Won't be able to tell the difference."

They started forward. As they walked the sky grew darker, and as the sky grew darker they started to see the faint lights of the buildings of the City of Night. As they got closer still, they could hear the noise. It sounded like someone was composing a car accident.

Chapter 13

It got dark all at once. It was not an oh-isn't -it-pretty-when-the-sun-goes-down kind of getting dark. It literally got dark *all at once.* Christian and Faith stepped over the line that marked the city boundary and immediately it was night. They were two feet from where they had been standing.

They both turned around and looked back down the road they had just traveled. It was night there behind them too.

"That was weird," Faith said. She started to turn around and Christian caught her arm.

"Where are you going?" he asked.

"I want to see if it will be daylight when I step back."

"I think we should just keep going," he said. She looked behind her at the sky that had previously been daylight and said, "You could be right."

It was a simple conversation but both of them were thinking the same thing: that if Faith stepped over the city line again and into the daylight it would seem like a thousand-mile distance between them. Neither wanted that.

In front of them lay the straight and narrow path but now it was as wide as a highway. A flashing neon sign read "Welcome Back My Friends to the Show that Never Ends! We're

So Glad You Could Attend! Come Inside! Come Inside!" And in very small letters beneath that it read "Zoned for your protection."

"You think that's the name of the city or the 'Mission Statement'?" Faith asked.

"I saw this place featured on 'Where Not To Live,'" Christian said.

"You're kidding," Faith said.

"Yes," Christian said. He started walking and Faith looked at the back of his head and then followed.

There was no way to tell if it was night or day outside of the city. Looking back toward the city limits, Christian could see no trace of the previous day. It was fully night inside and outside of the City of Night.

As they walked, people came out of the shops that lined either side of the road. They came up to the edge of the path and held out what they were selling. A man had DVDs and CDs hanging from his coat. "Latest releases," he said. "Not available in stores yet. $20."

Another man held out a necklace. "Buy your girlie-girl something pretty."

They didn't look. Faith reached out and held his hand as they walked. "Just keep your eyes straight ahead," she said. "We can walk right through this."

Off to the left of them a house with a large balcony stood dark. As they got closer, the light in the second floor window came on. Two girls wearing what in some states would be considered clothing (in others it might be considered postage) came out and leaned over the balcony. "We've got what every boy wants," they called to Christian. Christian kept his head forward and allowed his eyes to drift toward the young ladies on the balcony.

Faith spotted this move and said, "Guys are such pigs."

Christian shrugged, and she pulled him along.

Dozens more poured out of houses and shops along the road, each seller walking right up to—but not onto—the straight and narrow path. Soon it became obvious. Faith said, "Why don't they walk up on the road. Are they scared?"

"Not scared," Christian said. "I think it only counts if we are lured off the path. As long as we stay on the path we should be perfectly safe."

Soon both Christian and Faith began to feel like the grand marshalls of a floatless parade. The people on the side of the road were four and five deep. Others were hanging out of windows. All of them had something to sell. All of them looking like their lives depended on the sale.

The farther they walked without buying anything, the angrier the crowds seemed to grow. Christian was suddenly struck by a full can of liquid. It slammed into the side of his head and exploded, sending out a spray of a sickeningly sweet soda. Christian fell to his knees and grabbed his head. "What the heck was that?"

Faith helped him to his feet. She checked the side of his head. "It's not bleeding."

"Feels like it should be," Christian said, rubbing it.

Faith pressed her hand against the mark and felt it getting warm beneath her hand. "It's going to swell up, I'm sure."

"We should keep moving," Christian said.

She nodded, but by that time the initial toss of the soda can had inspired the crowd, who promptly began throwing trash, food, and whatever they could get their hands on. Both Christian and Faith ducked their heads and covered them with their hands. They never let go of each other's hands as they began to run.

The shouts of the crowd grew louder, and a large tire landed in the path in front of them. It was on fire. Black smoke belched out of the center. Christian went to the left and Faith to the right and they let go of each other's hand for just a moment. Christian reached for her hand again, but he tripped and fell. Faith turned and came back for him. She bent low, and a broken bottle flew over her where her face had been and struck a man on the other side of the road, lacerating his face. The man screamed and put his hand over his eyes as blood poured through his fingers.

The sound of a siren broke over the roar of the crowd and many people began to run. But there was no room. People at the front of the crowd closest to the road were shoving and punching their way to get away from it. Each shove was met with a punch in return. Each punch was met with a harder fist. Eventually knives were produced and several screams were heard like that of the man who had his face gashed.

A man in a security uniform appeared and grabbed both Christian and Faith and hauled them to their feet. Ignoring the shouts and screams around him he put them both in the back of his car. Christian read the words on the outside of the cop car door: "Vanity Fare Creek: A Gated Community."

In the back of the security guard's car, Christian looked over at Faith. She had a small cut on her cheek and the side of her face was covered in some sort of muck that looked like it had been scraped from a garbage can. She said, "Your eye is swollen."

The patrol car bounced over something in the road and the driver swore. People slapped the windows on both sides of the vehicle.

The driver slammed the brakes and the two in the backseat were thrown forward against the front one. "*Move it, Junior!!*" The guard screamed. He hit the siren button again but the punching on the windows increased. Then the car began to rock back and forth.

The one eye that wasn't hurting grew wide. Christian said, "We're off the path." He had a vague awareness that they were turning upside down. He thought he heard Faith scream something, but it was covered by the sound of breaking glass.

*****

When Christian woke up, he wanted nothing more than to get a good lungful of air. But the duct tape across his mouth prevented him from getting one. It was identical to the tape that bound his hands to a vertical two-by-four wooden post. He looked around in the dim light. It appeared as if he was in a building that was undergoing renovation. There was very little light, except that of twelve television monitors that displayed a very weak white-noise pattern. They were arranged in two rows of five, one on top of the other.

He turned his head and saw Faith. She was awake but bruised. She saw him conscious and relief came to her eyes. She probably would have smiled, but she was bound the same way Christian was.

Behind them they heard a door open and the footsteps of heavy boots. Four men in uniforms, like that of the officer who had picked them up from the street, walked between them and stood nearby, two standing by each of the travelers.

A woman in an expensive suit and a pearl necklace took a seat in front of the twelve monitors. "Well, we have had a little disturbance, haven't we." She smoothed nonexistent wrinkles out of her dress and adjusted her perfect hair, which did not need adjusting.

The twelve monitors behind the woman suddenly flickered to life. Each one displayed a distorted image of a face. Beneath each face beamed yellow letters, which Christian assumed to be the names of those on the screen. There was:

C. Nothin

N. O'Good

M. Alice

2Sexy

O. Morles

G. Vibrait

B. Snobb

Ann Tagonist

U. Fibber

B. Cruell

D. Dark

M.T. Sole

Without looking away from Christian and Faith, the woman said, "Are we all here?"

The faces on the monitors spoke somewhat at the same time in a chorus of "All ready!" "Ready to go," "Present," and other variations on assent.

"Good," said the woman in the chair.

She nodded to one of the guards who, very gently at first, began to peel the duct tape off of Christian's face. Then, after a moment, he gave it one good yank. Christian was sure half his face had come with it.

"What do you have to say for yourself, young man?" the woman asked. She picked a non-existent piece of lint from her blouse.

"The guard," Christian said, "the one who helped us on the path, how is he?"

"Dead," the woman said. "But he was just a security guard. We have more of those."

Faith looked at the woman and tried to say something beneath the duct tape on her face, but it was unintelligible.

Another guard grabbed the tape on Faith's mouth and simply yanked it off. Faith said, "Uhhh!" and then spat on the ground. Christian could see there was blood in her spit.

"Let's start with your names," the woman said.

Christian said, "I am Christian. This is Faith. We are simply passing through."

"But you did not purchase anything," the woman said.

"We have no money," Faith said.

"Everyone has money," the woman said. That's how we survive. People sell. People buy. That's the way things are."

"We have no money," Faith repeated. "Check our bags. We didn't bring any money."

Christian looked around and just then realized he did not have the canvas bag that the Manager had given him. He saw it was now in the lap of the woman in the chair. She was rummaging through it. "Well, that's simply stupid," the woman said. "How can you expect to be a part of the economy without money? It's essential to keeping up our way of life."

"You call that a way of life?" Faith said. "People waving worthless crap at us and demanding money and getting violent when we don't buy anything?"

The woman nodded at one of the security guards, who stepped over and slapped Faith hard across the face.

"One does not question when one is a guest in someone's home, dear," the woman said in a singsong voice, like a kindergarten teacher.

The woman opened Christian's canvas bag and removed the Magic 8 Ball. She smiled. Shook it and turned it over. She frowned and put it back in the bag. She examined the iPods in both bags as if she had never seen one before. Then she pulled out the book that Christian had been carrying since he started this journey.

She thumbed through it and looked at Christian. "Prophecy?"

"In a manner of speaking," Christian said.

"Valuable?"

"Only to me."

She put the items back in the bags and handed the bags to one of the security guards. The guard took the bags and hung them around the necks of both Christian and Faith. The woman said, "You will have to answer for your crimes. I see no need to..."

"What crimes?" Faith yelled.

The guard stepped forward and this time backhanded Faith across the mouth. This time Faith spit blood on his shoe. "We've done nothing wrong."

"You came into our city without knowledge of its customs. You caused a riot with your ignorance. You questioned the authority of the governing body. You have been found to have no belongings of any worth."

"Nothing is of worth!" Faith said. Christian tried to catch her eye to make her shut up.

The dark face with the nose ring and the bejeweled teeth on the monitor marked 2Sexy appeared to lean closer to the screen. "Say that again."

"All that you have is your soul," Faith said. "It's all anyone really has. Everything else is meaningless."

The woman in the chair scowled.

Christian noticed the head of a nail sticking out of the two-by-four he was taped to. He began to work the tape back and forth across the metal edge of the nail.

The woman's face on the monitor marked O. Morles said, "Without property you can't put a value on a person. It is how we are defined."

There were nods of assent in the other monitors.

The face on the monitor marked B. Snobb spoke in a thick accent. "He who dies with the most toys...wins."

The others smiled as if he had just quoted an old and ancient law.

Faith said, "He who dies with the most toys...*still dies.*"

The smiles went away. The monitor face marked Ann Tagonist put her hand over her mouth. The bearded face in "C. Nothin" shouted *"Blasphemer!"*

The other faces in the other monitors began to repeat the word like a curse. As if the mere repetition would shield them from whatever it was that frightened them.

"Enough!" the Chairwoman said. "We have a witness."

From the dark shadows of the building a small man limped forward. He clutched his hat in his hand and looked at the floor. Christian looked at Faith. He saw her eyes widen. She turned to the Chairwoman. "This is your witness?"

The guard drew back and Faith glared at him as he struck her face again. This time she did not flinch.

"The witness may speak," the Chairwoman said.

"Madam Chairwoman," the old man said. "I own a small record store not too far from here. Not as fine as the businesses here, of course, but I get by. This young woman came into my home and tempted me and my daughter with her wanton ways."

"He's a perv," Faith said. For the first time there was a trace of worry in her voice. "He tried to molest his own daughter. She told me so."

The Chairwoman looked at the guard, who this time came forward with a roll of tape. He pulled a strip off and covered Faith's mouth.

"And the boy?" the face on the monitor labeled B. Cruell asked.

"I've never seen him," the old man said, "but if he was with the girl then she disrupted him, too."

"That isn't fair!" Christian said. "We're allowed to answer what charges are made against us."

This outburst was met with another strip of tape pulled tightly over his own mouth. Christian managed to pull his lips into his mouth so they did not feel like they would be torn off when the inevitable yanking happened.

"My daughter was a perfectly lovely young woman, respectful and helpful. The harlot came in and...she changed her...she made her...one of those."

There were gasps from the monitor faces. The Chairwoman said, "The witness is dismissed."

The old man said, "But there's more."

"We've heard enough."

"But my money!" the old man said.

Faith's eyes narrowed and she looked at the Chairwoman. The Chairwoman waved her hand and one of the security guards grabbed him by his collar and hauled him away.

"You!" the Chairwoman said to Faith. "You're on your way to the City of Light after what all those people have done to your kind over the years?"

Faith tried to speak but could not form words.

"The City of Light, where all the good little people live and all the bad little people are pushed out of the way? You *really* think they're going to embrace you with open arms? Why, you'll be lucky if they don't burn you at the stake."

Faith tried to speak again. The Chairwoman stepped down off her platform and walked toward Faith. She grabbed the tape and pulled hard. This time Faith spit in her face.

The woman slapped Faith. "You little whore! If you've infected me I'll have you killed."

"Too late!" Faith spat. "Welcome to the club."

Christian screamed from beneath the tape on his mouth. His eyes pleaded with her to stop.

The Chairwoman turned away.

"She has something of value."

The Chairwoman looked at the monitor of N. O'Goode. Even though the camera was on the wall she looked into the face on the monitor itself. "Explain."

"She can sell what she has," O'Goode said. "There are people who would pay for that."

The Chairwoman turned back and walked over to a table full of construction equipment. She picked up a three-foot piece of rebar and held it under Faith's chin. "What about it, harlot? Are you willing to join our little community of economic growth? Are you willing to sell what you've obviously been giving away?"

"He lied!" Faith said. "He's a perv. The only thing anyone has that is of any value in the long run is their soul. I'm not going to sell mine, to you or anybody else."

The Chairwoman drew back so fast that no one even saw her move. She whipped the rebar quickly and smashed it into the side of Faith's head. The side of her skull caved in and her neck snapped over with an audible and sickening crack. Faith's body slumped down, held up only by the duct tape on her wrists. Her head hung at an impossible angle and blood poured from the open wound.

Christian screamed from beneath the tape on his mouth. His eyes filled with tears. Whatever was left inside of his friend shifted and left. She was gone. He was alone.

The Chairwoman returned to her seat and looked at the spot of blood on her skirt. "Awwwwwwwww," she said. She licked her finger and tried to rub the stain out. "Members of the Board, how do you find the defendant?"

There was an awkward pause and one by one each of the faces on the monitors said, "Guilty," and blinked out.

Christian was leaning against the wooden post and sobbing.

One of the guards spoke up. "Madam Chairwoman, what about him?"

The Chairwoman was still rubbing the spot on her skirt and looked up as if she had forgotten all about Christian. "Hmmm? Oh." She waved him off, "Life in prison."

With that she stepped off the platform and walked into the shadows of the basement.

Three of the security guards followed her. The one remaining was a large man who walked quietly over to Christian. He said, "Are you going to give me trouble?"

Christian shook his head no.

The guard said, "I'm going to cut you loose and then retape your wrists and then take you to the station. "Are you going to be good?"

Christian eyes were burned with tears and his nose was running. He looked at Faith's lifeless body and nodded his head.

The security guard pulled a knife from his pocket and cut the tape holding Christian's wrists on the other side of the post. "Hold them out for me."

Christian did.

As the guard began to retape the wrists the roll of silver tape went round once… twice… on the third time Christian shoved the man as hard he could. The guard stumbled backward and tripped over Faith's lifeless body. Christian ran.

Blindly at first, into the dark, he tried to wipe his eyes with his hands and nearly lost his balance. The basement was dark. He heard the security guard yelling and struggling to his feet. Christian heard the sound of the city and ran toward it. He saw boards and pipes in the dark just before running into them. He heard the guard behind him run into something and swear loudly.

Christian found a door and threw it open. He was out and onto a city street. The cool air felt good on his skin. He was about to pull the tape from his mouth, but he saw headlights coming toward him. He tried to get a deep breath through his nose but he could not. He fell to his knees believing that this is where his journey would end. He would be a spot on the pavement that the Preacher would never know about.

The pickup truck swerved and missed him at the last second. A dark-skinned man with long dreads hung out the window of the truck and shouted, "Git in!"

Christian heard the door he had just come through bang open loudly and break off its hinges. He had no other choice. He stood and threw himself into the back end of the pickup truck like a high jumper throwing himself over the bar. There was no soft pad to land on. He landed on his arm and winced at the pain. He looked up at the night sky, which was covered in a thick black smog. Through a small opening he thought he saw one star.

The truck was already moving at a fast clip when he heard the small window that separated the bed and the cab of the truck slide open. A hand reached through the open window and pulled the tape from his mouth. It stung but the clean air felt so good in his lungs he didn't care. The man inside looked out at him. "Ya mon, be safe now. Ya' be safe. Yo wit de Hope Mon. Dey call me Michael Hope."

Christian was going to smile, but at that moment consciousness chose to leave him to his own thoughts.

Chapter 14

Christian slept in the back of Mike Hope's Truck for eight long unconscious hours. He had awakened once only long enough to be aware the truck was moving and that his hands had been cut free. Then he returned to a deep sleep.

When he woke up it was day, but he had no idea what time it was. The continuous darkness of the City of Night had thrown off his inner clock. He opened one eye and then the other, the second sending pain through his entire head. He was aware that he was using the canvas bag the Manager had given him as a pillow. He wondered where he was and how far off the path he had been taken. He wondered if he had dreamed the man with the island accent or if he was real. He wondered if somehow he was still in danger and should stay low in the bed of the truck and not raise his head. Not that he wanted to raise his head—just the light alone was making his head throb.

"Ya wake now, mon?" The voice was the same as he had heard last night. He rolled over on his back and saw the man with the dreads looking down at him. "Ya wake now," he said. It wasn't a question this time. "Boy been running from de bad place."

"You saved my life," Christian said.

"Right place. Right time," the man said. "We met las' night but ya don be rememberin' dat now. Name is Hope. Mike Hope."

He held out a dark rough hand that Christian shook weakly.

"I brought ya some icey for dat eye," Hope said. He held out a plastic bag filled with ice. Christian started to raise himself. "Slowly, mon."

Christian took the advice and moved slower. Still it felt like his brain was sloshing to the side of his head and was going to leak out his ears. He took the bag of ice and gingerly touched it to the side of his head and over his swollen eye. "I saw my friend murdered."

"Don be talkin' right now," Hope said. "Plenty o' time for dat later. Ya wan to rest and git you some coffee in you and den when ya ready you can tell Mike Hope all about it."

Christian sat in the back of the truck with the bag of ice pressed to his skull for about ten minutes until it felt like the ice was beginning to pool up in the bag. Finally he lifted his face and looked around. They were in the parking lot of a Starbucks.

"I'm off the path," Christian said, and he again felt a deep sorrow.

"One journey. Many paths," Mike Hope said.

"Why did you pick me up?" Christian said.

"Wasn't meanin' to," Hope said. "De whole town be buzzin' about de two new commers. Say dey get caught by the association. Nobody gets away from de association. Lots of noise in the city and I decide it be a good time to make my escape too. You see somebody lying in de street with de hands and de mouth with de silver tape and you don do the drive by."

"They killed my friend," Christian said. He started to cry again.

"Dey kill a lot of people's friends," Hope said. "But dey don't kill you and dey don't kill Mike Hope."

"My name is Christian."

"Good name," Hope said. "You want some coffee and de sweet roll now." Again, this wasn't a question. Hope unhitched the gate of the pickup and Christian scooted himself toward it. "Don be fast," Hope said.

Slowly Christian swung his feet down and then pushed himself off the gate. Mike Hope caught him when he nearly lost his balance. "I need my bag," Christian said.

Mike Hope put Christian's hand on the edge of the truck so he could steady himself. Then he retrieved the canvas bag and looped it over Christian's head and shoulder.

"Thanks," Christian said.

"You good to walk now?" Hope asked.

"Yeah," Christian said, but he wasn't at all sure that he was.

The cool air and the aroma of coffee wafted over them as they went in. There was a faint smell of muffins and chocolate. "Heaven better smell dat good or I might not go in," Hope said. Christian did not feel like smiling. "You go sit in de booth and I'll bring sum-ting strong and black like Mike Hope," Hope said.

"Strong and black with cream and sugar," Christian said. Mike Hope smiled.

He walked away and Christian saw he was wearing a large baggie shirt with a print like that of the staff he had left behind at the mall. Christian wondered if Mike Hope had been to the Palace. He wondered if Mike Hope had met Mr. Watchman.

When Mike Hope returned, he was carrying a tray with coffee and two very large blueberry muffins. "Can't be heaven we in," Hope said. "Dey say de chocolate muffins not ready for another 20 minutes. In heaven I tink you git chocolate muffin whenever you want. So dis is not heaven. It's just a nice place for coffee."

Christian sipped his coffee, but only looked at the muffin in front of him.

"Dey come close to killin' you, dinna dey," Hope said quietly.

Christian looked into his rescuer's face for the first time. Mike Hope had long dreads and a small soul patch beneath his lower lip. His eyes were behind a pair of rimless glasses. They seemed ancient.

"They were going to put me in jail for the rest of my life," Christian said. "I watched a woman beat my friend to death."

Hope nodded. "Dis friend of yours. She be a girl?"

Christian nodded. "But not like what you're thinking?"

"How do you know what I'm tinkin'?" Hope said. "You sittin' dere and can't even tink straight yourself."

"She was my friend," Christian said.

"Ah," Mike Hope said. "And she be a nice girl with short hair and wrist bands and de black jeans and de funny shirt?"

Christian suddenly got worried. "You were there?"

"No," Hope said, "I was in de street and saw the riot as the opportunity to leave. Not everybody in the City of Night is de bad bad. Some just don't know when to leave."

"How did you know about my friend, Faith?"

Mike Hope pointed a long brown finger at the cup Christian was drinking from. Christian turned it around and saw a drawing had been printed on the cup. It was clearly a draw-ing of Faith. She was dancing on a cloud and next to her was a drawing of Jesus, who was also dancing. They were sur-rounded by what appeared to be a multitude of the heavenly host—who were also dancing. Beneath the printed drawing was the phrase "All that you have is your soul."

Christian started to cry, mostly from relief, but partially because he missed his friend. "Mine's a quote from Mr. Mark Twain," Hope said as he broke off a piece of his muffin and ate it. Christian sipped his coffee and felt better. Twenty minutes later his headache was gone and the light had returned to his eyes.

"Your friend," Mike Hope said, "She git dere before you. Her journey is done. You still got more to learn apparently."

Christian said, "You want to come?"

Hope said, "You askin cause you want me to come along wit you or you askin me cause I got a car?"

"I'm asking because the journey is long and it's harder to do alone."

"Den I come wit you," Hope said. "Take you time. It's still early day. We can go when you done wit you girly-coffee." He smiled at Christian, who couldn't help himself and smiled back. He ran his thumb along the drawing of Faith on his cup.

*****

Four men came into the little coffee shop. If any one of them had come in to rob the place and *if* that individual had absconded with a bag full of cash from the register and *if* the police had asked the witnesses to describe the perpetrator... the same description would have fit all four. Tall. White. 30's. Businessman's haircut. White shirt. Grey pants. Little blue gizmo clipped to his ear. The only difference in the general description of the four men would have been in the variations of the color red in their neckties.

They came in from the parking lot striding with great purpose. This wasn't a coffee. This was a meeting. Each held a black notebook, which they tucked under their left arm as they took their coffees to the small bar and added cream.

The Starbucks was empty accept for Christian and Mike Hope, but the four men chose to sit in the table right next to the pair. They moved their chairs loudly, they sat roughly, they passed the small table service rack around the table once, each handing it to another, before someone reached over and placed it on a empty table. They all opened their black notebooks and were soon engrossed in deep meeting language. As was the custom, the barristers had written the names of the customers on the white cardboard cups. The four men were

Byron

Aaron

Cash

Horde

Christian and Mike Hope looked at the "event" that was happening before them. Hope turned to Christian and whispered, "Mon, dat was reelly reelly white."

Christian smiled and put his head in his hand. The two sipped their coffees and listened to the meeting next to them.

"Merchandise," one of them said as if announcing the arrival of a dignitary. "What's available?"

"You name it," said another. "T-shirts, hoodies, cups, rubber wrist bands, travel mugs, journals, pens...."

"Hoodies," said another. "Kids like hoodies."

"More than T-shirts?"

"Our research shows two to one in favor of hoodies," said the fourth man. His name was actually Cash. Christian could see that his laptop screen was a spreadsheet. He was using his pencil eraser to tap the keys.

"We can do both," said the first man. "We sold out of almost everything last year. People were asking for more stuff."

"I'm wondering," said another, "does it count as merchandising if it has a cross on it?"

"Do we make a profit?" said Cash.

"Yes."

"Then it's merchandising."

The first man who spoke said, "It's evangelism."

"If you don't use it for evangelism, it's merchandising."

"It could be unintentional evangelism. People still see the cross and God can still speak to them through it."

The others, who had stopped working to ponder the idea, resumed making notes.

"But," said Aaron (his last name was Gance), "Is it right for someone who is not from our church to sell our stuff? Can an atheist store owner sell one of our T-shirts?"

"Do we make a profit?" Cash asked.

The others smiled. "Presumably," said Byron.

"Then it all goes back to the church. Doesn't matter who sells it."

The rest of the table seemed satisfied with this answer and resumed making meeting notes.

There was a moment of "group jotting." Then Mr. Horde said, "But..."

The others simultaneously lifted their fingers off their keyboards.

"Another way to look at this is that a good businessman gets blessed by God in the form of profits from selling religious items, and is therefore inherently religious because God has blessed him regardless of whether he thinks of himself as a religious person or not."

Cash said, "Jesus equals profit."

They all nodded and resumed typing.

Christian looked over at Hope in disbelief. He whispered, "Did I just hear that right?"

Mike Hope just quietly shook his head.

Byron said, "So what's our convention swag?"

"We put the RTRJ logo on everything in the catalog," Cash said.

Christian finally spoke up. "I'm sorry. I didn't mean to eavesdrop, but what is RTRJ?"

"Real Teens for a Real Jesus." The group of four men said it like a mantra.

"Is dat a band?" Hope asked.

"It's a movement," Horde said.

"Ah," Hope said and looked at Christian with a what-the-hell-does-that-mean look.

"You've heard of us. Haven't you, son?" Byron said. "Real Teens for a Real Jesus?" He said it as if repeating made it clearer.

Christian looked at him blankly.

"We had thirty Teen Youth Jams in twenty States last year. Thousands of teens came out and decided to be Real Teens for a Real Jesus."

"And the RTRJ is your catchphrase?" Christian asked.

"It's our logo," said the man whose name was Aaron Gance. He spun his laptop around and there on the screen was a blue hoodie with a yellow RTRJ on the front.

"Nice," Christian said. "What else does it come on?"

Cash smiled. "Hoodies, T-shirts, sweatpants, cell phone covers, pens, laminated lanyards, coffee mugs, travel mugs, baseball caps, pins, collectable backscratchers, scarves, our own personal line of RTRJ Ready-To-Drink energy drinks. We call those "Christ & Caffeine." And of course the CDs and DVDs of our conventions."

"No mouse pads?" Christian asked.

"*Mouse pads!*" Byron said, slapping his forehead. "Write that down."

Horde tapped his keyboard. "Already on order."

The man whose name was Byron Gitwonfrie turned back to Christian. "Say, son... you're obviously a Real Teen for a Real Jesus. Would you wear a hoodie or a T-shirt with our logo?"

Christian said, "Most of the guys in my school who would wear an RTRJ logo on their shirt would get beat up by the guys who wear black T-shirts with synonyms for death on them."

The men at the table nodded. Some of them looked like it was from personal experience.

"Funny thing is..." Christian said, "the people that Jesus seemed to have the most contempt for were the ones that followed him around for the loaves and fishes."

The rest of the table stopped typing and looked over at the teenager with the black eye.

"Then there were the Pharisees," Christian continued. "Jesus warned people about being like them because they wore their faith like a hoodie. They prayed in public so people would see how religious they were. Oh, and don't think that because you're a businessman who hangs out with Christians that you're making God happy. Anybody remember Judas?"

Christian raised his hand like he was asking for volunteers. "Judas? Hello? Guy who kept the money and betrayed Christ? Anyone? Anyone?"

"Uhhhh...." Byron started.

"And," said Christian "wouldn't someone who finds religion for the sake of making a profit be just as likely to toss it away for the same reason?" Christian looked down at his cup. The picture had changed. The drawing of Faith was now looking at him and laughing.

"I'm not sure you *are* a Real Teen for a Real Jesus," Horde said.

"What is a *real* teen?" Christian asked. "For that matter, what is a *real* Jesus? Is there a fake Jesus out there that I don't know about?"

Byron Gitwonfrie reached into his pocket and placed two tickets on the table in front of Christian and Mike Hope. "If you two would like to come to the Real Teen Real Jesus concert tonight, it's on me." Christian looked down at the passes.

"I don't know," Christian said. "What would Jesus do?"

Christian decided that was a much better exit line than "Very Christian of you" and he glanced at the picture on his coffee cup to see if Faith was laughing, but the picture had returned to the one of her doing the happy dance with Jesus.

Mike Hope looked at Christian and said, "You ready to travel again?"

Christian nodded. He looked over at the Real Teens for a Real Jesus marketing team, but they were already engrossed in their notes and laptops again. He emptied the coffee cup and looked at the side again. The picture of Faith was now simply a quote from Tom Hanks. Whatever Faith had wanted him to know she had already told him.

He pitched the cup in the garbage can as they left. Mike Hope climbed into the driver seat and Christian crawled in the other side. "Do you know where we are going?" Christian asked.

"De City of Light," Hope said.

"And you know how we get there?"

"Second star to de right and straight on until de mornin'."

"Works for me," Christian said.

*****

About thirty minutes down the road a hand-painted wooden sign said, "See the tree where Judas hung himself." Beneath that in small letters someone with a steadier hand had painted "Fresh Cookies."

"Any desire to see de tree where de Judas-mon hung hisself?" Mike asked.

"I didn't realize that was around here."

"De probably moved it from Jerusalem."

"Then again, has anything on your journey made sense? I mean in a real-world kind of way?"

Mike Hope was silent.

"I'm sorry," said Christian. "I wasn't prying. Your journey is your business."

"I not ready to talk about me journey yet, mon. Even so, I tink stoppin' to see de death tree is de wrong way to go."

"Maybe we'll drive past the world's largest ball of twine," Christian said.

"Now dat I would like to stop and see," Hope said. Christian wished again that Faith were here. She and Mike Hope would have gotten on very well. He pushed the image of her death from his mind and filled it with the image of her doing the happy dance with Jesus.

The pair drove past the sign and into the day. Twenty or thirty minutes behind them, the marketing team from Real Teens for a Real Jesus pulled off the side of the road and parked. They walked the quarter mile back to the edge of a high cliff where an old tree stood with its strongest branch extended out over the drop.

"Amazing how they preserved it," Byron said.

"We should take pictures," Aaron Gance said. "Maybe we can work it into the brochure somehow."

"Wonder why they don't charge admission?" Cash said.

Horde began to speak, but at that moment the ground beneath their feet gave way and all four plummeted to the rocks below.

Chapter 15

Mike Hope drove the pickup down the road between rolling hills and trees on either side of the road. They had not seen a house or a business for miles. Up ahead they saw another hand-painted sign. This one read:

"See Lot's Wife! The Pillar of Salt! Just one more mile."

Christian turned to Mike Hope. "C'mon! You know you've always wondered what she looked like."

Mike Hope shook his head. "Don' need to know."

Christian said, "But this is the second Biblical tourist attraction we've passed. Maybe we're supposed to learn something."

Sighing, Mike Hope pulled into the right lane and prepared to take the turnoff to see Lot's Wife. He turned right onto a barely paved side road and eased the pickup over the hill. There was a round building with a lighted sign that said

Lot's Wife Tourist Center

There were no cars in the small parking lot. Mike got closer and said, "Maybe Mrs. Lot not be in de house today. Nobody is here."

"The sign says Open," Christian said, pointing to a plastic "Yes We Are Open" sign in the window.

Hope parked and the two got out and wandered toward the building. They opened it and were met with a blast of cool air. Shutting the door behind them they wandered in. "Helloooooooooooooooo?" Mike Hope sang.

The lights came on and there in the center of a large open room was a museum display blocked off by velvet ropes. The room itself was clean and carpeted but the display was designed to look like rocky soils just outside of Sodom. In the center was a statue that certainly looked as though it could have been made of salt. Both Christian and Mike Hope thought about touching it, but neither wanted to cross into the display.

The statue depicted a woman who was running in one direction and clearly looking in another. On a small stand was a red plastic button. Christian pushed it and at once the lights in the room dimmed, except for those lighting the display. A chorus of angry voices began to sing and the deep voice of James Earl Jones began to read the story of the destruction of Sodom and Gomorrah. After the reading, the chorus stopped and the lights in the room came back on.

"Well, that was fun," Christian said.

"You tink dere would be refreshments or some'ting," Mike Hope said.

Outside, Christian said, "You want me to drive?"

Mike Hope tossed him the keys and in a minute they were back on the highway. Mike Hope looked out the window and said nothing for a long time. Christian began to grow uneasy with the silence and finally said, "So what's the lesson of Lot's wife?"

"She be a stupid woman," Hope said.

"What do you mean?"

"I mean she get de easiest of instructions. Run. Don't look back. She couldn't follow dose and now she a tourist attraction."

"Ah," Christian said.

"Easy instruction," Mike repeated. "God say he gonna destroy the city. Gonna bring down the fire, but he choose Lot and his family to rescue because dey good people and den she look back and get all salty."

"So the lesson is about not looking back?" Christian asked.

"De lesson," Mike Hope said, "is don be stupid. When God hands you a present de best ting to do is follow de instructions."

Christian guessed that the whole stopover itself was for Mike Hope. Whatever journey he was on was now a shared one. They were traveling together and would experience things together.

They drove for another four hours until the sun was starting to set. They passed a large billboard that said

REST

That was all.

There was a second billboard another mile up the road that said

COMFORTABLE BEDS

"Do we stop for a hotel?" Christian asked.

"Don't know if we supposed to," Mike said. "I been sleepin in the back of de truck."

Another mile. Another billboard. This one read:

YES, MIKE. YOU CAN STOP HERE.

Christian and Mike Hope looked at each other but didn't say anything.

Another Billboard. Another mile. This one said:

FREE PIE

"Okay, dat do it for me," Hope said.

"Not the one with your name on it but the one that said FREE PIE?" Christian asked.

"Long story," Mike Hope said. "Pull off."

Another mile and around the turn was a huge flashing neon sign that read "The Quiet Waters Motel," over what looked like a two-room building.

The vacancy light was lit and beside the hotel was the world's largest ball of twine.

*****

Inside the "lobby" was a small counter and an open registration book. Beyond was a key rack with just two keys, one labeled "Room 1" and the other "Room 2." A large cooler with a sliding glass door and a Coca-Cola sign on the top was filled with various kinds of pie. Another cooler was filled with cold drinks, including chocolate milk, coffee, sodas and juices. The pie cooler, the soda cooler, the registration book, and the key rack all had the same handwritten sign: "Self-Serve."

There were two plates, two forks, two easy chairs and one radio that was playing Miles Davis. Christian and Mike Hope did not ask questions. They ate two slices of pie each and then simply took their keys from the rack and said their good nights. Christian's room was furnished with a large king-size bed and homemade quilts. There were six pillows and a nightstand stocked with various books. Two chairs and his own bathroom that was spotless and furnished with all manner of soaps and shampoos.

He showered and shaved. Stepping out, he noticed a set of clean cotton PJs in his size. He dressed, and in his room he found a back door that he hadn't noticed before. It spilled out onto a patio with a hot tub and a pool. Mike Hope was in the hot tub.

Christian walked over. "We can't stay here, can we."

"Nah, mon. We can't."

"Couple a days though, right?" Christian asked.

"Seems we got invited to stay. I guess we will be invited to go away when de time comes." Mike Hope slunk a little lower in the tub.

Christian was going to open his mouth and say something that was on his mind, but he chose to keep it shut. He saw how relaxed Mike Hope was and he didn't want to spoil it. What he was thinking was this...every time he had been given a nice place to stop and rest...it meant that something very very hard was around the corner.

*****

They stayed for two more days. Each morning there was hot coffee and fresh baked goods in the lobby. Each noontime, sandwiches and soups appeared, and at night, fresh, hot but not extravagant dinners. Mike Hope moved the radio that played only Miles Davis out to the patio. Christian found a dozen books by his favorite author, including several that he didn't know existed.

On the fourth morning, Christian woke because of the cold. He reached for the blanket, but it was gone.

He opened one eye and then the other and saw that the room had changed. The curtains were gone, as was the furniture. He swung his feet over the edge of the bed and discovered the carpet had vanished, leaving only cold wooden boards.

He slipped off the bed and already had a good idea of what waited for him out in the lobby. The room was empty now and dirty. The radio was gone and Christian could see through the window to the pool out back, which was now dry.

Mike Hope had beaten him to the lobby by only a minute or two. There on the counter were two plates, each with one slice of pie wrapped in plastic wrap. And there were two brown lunch bags, each with the name of the intended carrier.

Mike Hope looked at Christian and quietly said, "I tink dis is our invitation to be goin."

*****

After they had dressed and began walking toward the truck Christian said, "I wonder if they filled the gas tank."

"They" had.

They stopped at noon and ate their bag lunches under a tree. Mike Hope drove with his fingers drumming to the Miles Davis tune that was still in his head. About three o'clock in the afternoon he said, "Hello. What is dis?"

Christian looked at him. He was looking in the rearview mirror. Christian turned around and for the first time since his journey started he saw another car on the road. This one was coming up fast. In a few minutes it overtook the pickup and slid in front of them.

Neither caught a glimpse of the sports car's driver. He had a vanity plate that said #1. In his back window someone had painted in white letters "City of Light or Bust."

"We close," Mike Hope said, smiling. "We must be close. We just follow de man in the nice-nice and then we get there, maybe today."

Christian said, "He has a vanity plate that says #1."

Mike Hope looked at him questioningly.

"A *vanity* plate that says number *one*—isn't that a double whammy of how not to approach the City of Light?"

Mike Hope looked back at the car he was speeding to catch up to.

Christian said, "Plus, he's announcing to the world that he's on this journey. Aren't we supposed to keep this kind of quiet? Isn't that asking for trouble?"

Mike Hope said, "We agree dat we go on this part of the journey together. The mystery Manager at de Palace tinks we should be traveling together. So we make dis decision together. What you want to do?"

Hope was still speeding to keep up with the sports car.

Christian sighed and said, "We spotted him while you were behind the wheel. That must mean something. If your first instinct is to follow him, then let's do that."

Mike Hope followed the sports car for another hour. Once he tried to pull up next to the car so that Christian could get a good look at the driver, but when he did the sports car moved faster. Hope had the truck up to eighty-five when it started to shimmy and shake. He eased it back down to seventy and the shimmying stopped. But the car was further away.

They passed a fork in the road. It was the first "choice" they had come to since starting out that day. The road off to the left seemed old and rocky. Hope kept the truck on the highway and followed the sports car.

The sports car nearly flew over the next hill. When the truck crested the hill, Christian screamed, "*Stop!!!!!!!*"

A hundred feet away the highway ended. It simply stopped and dropped off into an abyss. Both men in the truck saw the taillights of the car go over the edge. Hope stomped on the brake, throwing Christian into the dashboard. The truck screamed in protest and finally stopped a foot from the edge. Both men then heard the explosion as the sports car slammed into whatever was at the bottom of the abyss.

Christian pushed himself back on the seat and looked at Mike Hope. Mike was gripping the steering wheel and panting.

"Back us up," Christian said.

Hope slid the truck into reverse and eased it backward, barely going fast enough for it to be considered movement. The truck crested the hill behind them and coasted back down into the gully between the hills. The engine then coughed once, twice, and died.

Both men got out of the truck at the same time and ran toward the edge of the cliff. A column of smoke was already rising into the air from deep down in the pit. They got as close to the edge as they could, but still could not see the bottom.

They turned and walked back toward the truck.

"Can you fix a truck?" Christian asked.

"No," Mike Hope said. "Can you?"

"No," Christian said.

Then it started to rain.

*****

They sat in the cab of the truck for a long time and listened to the sound of the rain. Finally Mike Hope said, "Dere's a knife in de glove box. You hand it to me, pleeze?"

Christian opened the glove box and found the Swiss army knife and handed it to Mike Hope. Hope opened his brown paper sack and pulled out the apple he had not eaten at lunch. He used the knife and cut it half and gave half to Christian. "Thanks," Christian said.

"I'm sorry," Mike Hope said.

"For what?"

"For following the driver with the vanity plates. I should have known better."

"You think we'll make any more mistakes as we go along, or is that going to be the last one for both of us ever?"

Hope said, "I suspect we make a few more along de way."

Christian bit into the apple, "Then I suspect you don't need to be sorry."

They waited for the rain to stop. It didn't . When Mike Hope realized that the gully the truck was sitting in was starting to flood, he said, "I think we may be getting wet."

When it became obvious that the rain wasn't going to let up

and the truck wasn't going to start, the two men packed what they could and stepped out of the truck—into water that sloshed up over their shoes.

"We could run and get wet," Christian said, "or we could walk and get wet. How far back was that turnoff?"

"A ways," Mike said, as his dreads started to stick together.

"You couldn't be more specific?"

"I was following the vanity plates trying to get us killed, remember?"

They walked in the rain with their heads down and their jackets pulled closed. Eventually they arrived at the spot where the road separated, and this time took the one that sloped downward. Water rushed past their feet.

Even in the dark they spotted the giant purple gorilla.

Christian saw it first in the distance. He stopped in his tracks. Mike Hope looked at him and then turned to see what he was looking at. In the far distance the giant purple gorilla stood, being blown back and forth by the wind and the rain.

It was a girl gorilla. She wore a bright green leopard-spotted sundress that hung down past her giant knees. In her hands she held a giant vinyl sign that read "DESPAIR MOTORS." The inflatable beast seemed to wave them over, but that was just a trick of the wind.

Running now, the pair crested the next hill and veered off the road and across a field to the auto dealership where the giant purple temptress leaned with the wind. There was a small shack that offered no protection from the rain at all. Christian and Mike Hope banged loudly on the door. When no one came, Christian said, "I bet it's dry under that sundress."

Mike Hope said, "I'm not standing under the sundress of a giant purple inflatable gorilla."

Christian said, "C'mon. Just don't look up."

The green sundress hung down nearly the ground. Beneath it the grass was mostly dry and the air smelled like a beach ball. It was like hiding in a big plastic tent.

Christian sat and Mike Hope did too. "You remember that scene in *Forest Gump* where they sat back to back so that neither would have to sleep in the mud?"

Mike Hope scooted around so he was back to back with Christian. "As I recall," Hope said, "de next day de black man die in dat movie."

"He wasn't from the island," Christian said.

Hope leaned back against Christian. "Dat don't give me no nice-nice."

"It's all I got," Christian said. "I need to work on my exit lines."

They both slept, though not at the same time and not for more than five minutes at a shot.

When the light of the morning was shining through the grape ape's sundress, Christian and Mike Hope stood and moaned at their stiff joints. They stepped under the vinyl flap and were met by a very round man with a very large shotgun. "Think you can steal one of my cars, do ya? Well let me tell you, you cain't. Nobody steals my cars."

Christian looked at Hope. Mike Hope said "Sorry" again.

"Sir," Christian said. He rubbed his hands together and said, "We had a bit of car trouble ourselves up the road and when it started to rain we took shelter under your...your...uh..."

"That there's a point o'sale advertising display," the man said. He motioned toward the gorilla with the shotgun.

"Does it work?" Mike Hope asked.

"Course it works. Customers will be coming in anytime now."

Christian said, "Well, we wish you luck with your sale. We'll be on our way."

The man leveled the shotgun at the pair. "I don't believe I gave you permission to leave yet. How do I know you wasn't planning to steal one of my cars?"

Hope said, "He just told you. We were just lookin' to stay dry."

"And you just happened to take shelter under the skirt of my gorilla," the man said. "You 'spect me to believe that?"

"It's the truth," Christian said.

"Round my dealership," the man said, "truth depends on who's doing the sellin'."

Christian and Mike Hope were led through the showroom of Despair Motors and through a back door into the garage. There were eight work bays, each one abandoned. "Had to close up the garage and let my mechanics go for financial reasons," Denny Despair said.

The work bay in the center of the garage was for changing oil filters. It was a six-foot pit in the floor, deep enough for a grown man to stand and be able to reach up into the underbelly of a car and change the oil filter. From the outside it looked much deeper than six feet.

Denny Despair pointed the gun at Christian and spoke to Mike Hope. "Okay, Mr. Rastaman, over there on the workbench you'll find some handcuffs and some chains. Would you mind going and getting those for me? If you don't feel obliged to do that I'll blow your friend's head off."

Mike Hope made no expression on his face as he walked toward the workbench. Christian looked at Denny Despair and said, "Can I ask why you just happen to have handcuffs in the garage?"

"Can't trust nobody," Despair said. "We're way out of the way out here, takes the cops forever. Man has a right to protect what's his."

Mike Hope returned with the chains and handcuffs. Despair said, "Now gentlemen, if you'll just step back a moment." Despair walked over to the wall where a series of long metal poles stood. Each one was fifteen feet tall. Despair grabbed one with his free hand and pulled until the pole began to tip. Finally it fell and slammed into the garage's concrete floor. Despair kicked the pole with his heavy boot and it rolled until it stretched across the oil pit.

"Now, boys. If you'll put them there handcuffs on and step down in the pit I'll be calling the authorities to have you arrested."

Christian looked at Mike Hope, who was looking at Denny Despair's big gun. The two young men slowly eased themselves down into the pit. Denny Despair walked over and with his boot he shoved the chain over to the hole. "Take the chain and loop it through the cuffs, then throw it over the bar."

Mike and Christian did as they were told. The bar was long enough to prevent them from turning it or trying to flip one end of it into the pit. Denny Despair went over to his workbench and found a padlock the size of his hand. He locked the chain in place so that Christian and Hope had about seven feet of chain between them.

"There now," Denny Despair said. "I'm going to go and reassure the Missus that things are safe and sound and call the police."

"We just wanted to stay dry," Christian said one last time, but Denny Despair was already on his way out of the garage.

Christian and Mike Hope worked on the handcuffs and the chain for fifteen minutes. Hope said, "Dis is like one of dos puzzles dey give you at the restaurant to give you sometin' to do while you wait for you food."

Christian said, "I think he's done this before."

Hope raised his hands giving Christian as much slack as he could. There was enough chain for one of them to sit down and lean against the wall while the other stood with his hands in the air.

"We'll have to explain things to the police when they get here," Christian said.

Denny Despair went into his house and didn't come back out to the garage for three days.

Chapter 16

When Denny Despair walked into the house on that first day his wife was watching from the kitchen window.

"Did you lock them up?"

"Yes," Despair said.

"Did you put them down in the pit and use the big chain?"

"Yes," Despair said.

"Did you tell them you were going to call the police?"

"*Yes!*" Despair said. He said it louder, but his tone already sounded defeated.

"You have to do it." She scowled. "People these days will steal you blind."

"I know," Denny said. He poured himself a cup of coffee and sat down at the kitchen table.

"You going to do what you always do?"

"Yes," Denny said. He wasn't really listening anymore. His ears picked up the empty space in her speech and he simply said "Yes."

"Can't trust anyone," she said. She had not taken her eyes off the garage, thinking that at any moment the doors would blow off in an explosion and the two young men would come charging the house with knives and pistols. She had already imagined this so she knew it was true. "Just protecting ourselves."

"Yes," Denny said. He was reading Marmaduke in the comics. He tried not to smile because she would ask him what he was reading and then he would tell her and she would demand to know why he thought that was funny.

She busied herself in the kitchen glancing out the window every few minutes. "They've escaped," she said.

"I used the pole and the chain," he said. "They didn't escape."

After two days she said, "You know we can't let them go. They'll tell someone."

"I know it," Denny Despair said. They were eating lunch. Grilled cheese sandwiches and tomato soup.

"You're going to have to do something about it."

"I know it," Despair said.

"When?"

"Tomorrow."

She went back and looked at the garage through the window. She felt better knowing that the situation would be taken care of.

In the garage, Christian and Mike Hope hung from the pole by the handcuffs, barely strong enough to stand. They had not eaten since they left the little hotel with the free pie. When they had finally realized that Denny Despair wasn't coming back with the police, they devised a system where they could take turns sleeping and standing. Now they both simply hung from the pole.

"You boys tired yet?" Despair called out.

"We—" Christian started and realized that his throat was so dry he could barely speak. "We have to go. You can't keep us.

We're not animals."

"I don't intend to keep you like this," Denny said. "I'm going to kill you."

Mike Hope, who had hung for three days by his wrists and had already urinated on himself more than once, looked at Denny Despair with weak eyes.

"But I thought that I'd let you do the job yourselves." From his big coat pocket Despair pulled a large bottle of insecticide. He set it on the edge of the pit. "Take yourselves a big drink. I understand it burns a bit, but you'll be gone in ten minutes. Or if you feel you don't have the stones to do it yourselves, I can come back tomorrow and shoot you." Despair turned on his heel and began to walk away.

"Sir," Christian managed to say.

Denny Despair came closer and held his gun tighter.

"We'll take our own lives," Christian said. Mike Hope looked at him as if to say "Speak for yourself, white boy," but he didn't make any noise.

"Under the gorilla where you found us is a canvas bag. It has the tools of our worship. Allow us to worship our God one last time and in the morning you can come back and bury our bodies."

Despair considered this. "Seems like it'd be the Christian thing to do," he said more to himself than to the two men who were chained in the oil pit in his service garage.

Despair went out to the gorilla and peeked under the green dress. There in the grass was a canvas bag soaked with dew. He reached in and picked it up with the end of his shotgun. He carried it back to the garage as if he were afraid to touch it.

He lowered the bag into the pit. Mike Hope gave Christian some slack and Christian took the bag. He pulled out the book that had started this journey. He dropped the bag to his feet and waved the book at the salesman. "Thank you. We won't trouble you further."

Despair turned on his heel and walked away.

Inside the house his wife said, "What took you so long? Are they going to do it themselves or make you do it?"

"They'll do it," Despair said. "Least they said they would. They want to pray tonight and in the morning I'll pitch the bodies."

"You sure they know how to do it right?" she asked.

Denny Despair turned off his brain and simply said "Yes." Again.

*****

In the garage, Mike Hope looked at Christian and said, "You got a plan, right?"

They had been in the pit for three days without food, water or a toilet. Christian managed a weak smile and in a scratchy voice said, "Give me as much slack as you can."

Mike Hope raised his hands high and Christian bent down and picked up the bag. He put the book away and reached in the bottom of the bag. He smiled.

"What?" Mike Hope whispered.

Christian held up the key that the Manager had given him. It seemed like so long ago now. Christian grabbed Mike Hope's wrists and held the handcuffs tightly in one of his hands. He rubbed his thumb across the word "Promise" that had been engraved into the top of the key. "Here goes," he said.

Both men watched as the Promise key slid into the handcuff lock. The click was the most wonderful sound either of them had ever heard.

*****

Five miles away from Despair Motors, Christian and Mike Hope crawled on all fours to the top of a grassy hill. Neither had eaten or slept in three days. They reached the summit of the hill and lay on their backs staring at the night sky. "We're alive," Christian said, barely above a whisper. He said it to his friend and he said it to his God.

As if in answer, thunder rolled long and loud across the sky. The clouds opened and it began to rain.

*****

Neither made an attempt to move, though that was mostly from weakness.

They lay and let the rain wash them until it stopped. Then they lay there some more. It was nearly dawn when Christian sat up and groaned, wincing as he moved his shoulders. His wrists were raw and cut from the cuffs. As the sun came up he saw a strange silhouette in the distance.

"Hey, Hope."

Mike Hope opened his yes and looked at the indigo sky. He didn't move. "I was havin de dream where I am sleeping in my bed under de quilt my grandmamma sew for me out of de satin jackets a soccer team left in de hotel where she work."

Christian said, "You're on a hill. You just spent three days chained to a white boy in a garage and you smell."

"My dream was better," Hope said.

"What does that look like to you?"

"I not going to move. Describe it to me."

Christian said, "It looks like a parking garage. A very big one."

Mike Hope still had not moved. "Then let us say dat I trust

you judgment and what you be seein is, in fact, a very big parking garage."

"Fifteen or sixteen floors," Christian said.

"I trust you."

Christian said, "There's no city around it. It's just a parking garage."

Mike Hope pushed himself up to a seated position. His bones cracked like knuckles all over his body. "Uhhhhhhhhhhhhhh-hhh," he said.

Looking out in the distance, Mike Hope squinted in the dim morning light. What he saw certainly did look like a very large parking garage in the middle of nowhere.

"I would think," Christian said as he ran his fingers through his hair, "that if one was on, say...I don't know, a sacred journey of some kind, that a parking garage in the middle of nowhere might be something that the person or persons taking the journey would want to check out."

"You talk too much in de morning," Hope said. "Let's go."

Both young men groaned as they stood up. Mike Hope said, "I am barely twenty and my father didn't make that noise until he was sixty."

Christian laughed. "You never told me about your life, never said how you got started on this journey."

"Time for dat later," Hope said. "I am cold. I am hungry. I am hoping we find a nice kind person at de garage who can give us a donut."

They walked nearly a mile. The sun was fully up by the time they arrived. The dirt path they were walking on became blacktop. As they approached the garage they saw two men. One was in the booth where tickets and money are exchanged. The other man was standing just outside of the booth talking with the other. The man outside wore a bright orange vest with the word CAUTION on both sides. They looked up as the soaking wet, barely moving travelers approached.

Christian noted that there were no cars in the middle-of-nowhere parking garage. Both Christian and Hope were thinking that if these two guys knew Denny Despair of Despair Motors…they were screwed.

The man inside the booth leaned over and pressed the "talk" button he had inside the booth. His lips moved, but it was a speaker above the booth where his voice came from. "Help you gentlemen?"

Christian looked at Mike Hope and then back at the man in the booth. "We are on a journey. Sent by the Preacher. We are going to the City of Light. We were nearly killed by a man with a giant purple gorilla."

He said this and promptly fainted.

When he woke up he was laying on a cot in a small office. Mike Hope was sitting nearby. Mike Hope had been freshly showered and was wearing a pair of blue workman's coveralls. He was eating a donut. The room smelled like cheap coffee.

Mike Hope looked up from the book he was reading. "Coffee is ready."

Christian said, "Whoa. What happened?"

"You fainted," Hope said. "Caution caught you."

Christian shook his head. "What?"

Mike Hope stood and poured a coffee into an old Morning Edition coffee mug and handed it to Christian. "De big man wit de vest. His name is really Caution. You faint. He catch you before you bang you noggin."

"Where are we?"

"In de office," Hope said. "Batroom is right through dere. Take a shower. You feel better. You smell, white boy."

Christian made the decision that all of this would make a lot more sense if he simply did as he was told for the moment.

"Take dis," Hope said.

Christian turned and Mike Hope handed him a green garbage bag. Put you smelly clothes in it. We wash dem later."

Christian shuffled toward his seated friend and spotted a box of donuts on the desk. "Go 'head!" Mike Hope smiled.

Christian shoved a donut in his mouth, took the garbage bag from Hope's hand, clutched the coffee cup to his chest like a teddy bear, and shuffled toward the bathroom.

It was small but clean. Christian looked around for his donut and realized he had eaten it. His clothes peeled off him like the skin of a banana. He winced at his own smell. He dropped all his clothes into the green garbage bag, opened the door and dropped it outside. The hot water sprayed him in the head and seemed to melt away his aches and pains. He took the bar of soap, which smelled like industrial strength cocoa butter, and scrubbed himself all over. After twenty minutes the water started to run cold and he shut it off. He pulled back the curtain and a knock came at the door. "Don be nekid when I open de door, okay?" Hope called.

Christian pulled the curtain to cover himself. "All clear."

The door opened just enough for Hope to slip his arm through. He held out a towel, a pair of blue coveralls, and a plastic comb and tooth brush. Christian took these and laid them on the sink board. He dressed and then looked at himself in the mirror. He didn't remember the last time he'd looked at himself. He looked older than he remembered.

Stepping out into the office again, he saw Mike Hope sitting and reading from the book Christian kept in his backpack. This had a different cover. "Found it on de desk," Hope said. "Dese guys, de okay."

Christian nodded. "How long was I out?"

"Couple of hours," Hope said. "Come meet de boys."

Mike Hope stood up and the two of them left the office. Christian followed Hope because he had no idea where he was. They were both barefoot, but the concrete beneath them seemed new and spotless. Hope led Christian up a small incline and around a turn. The day was bright and Christian shielded his eyes.

"Hey! Look who's up! Good morning, sunshine!" The voice blared from the speaker in the booth.

Christian looked at the big man in the CAUTION vest.

"Morning people!" Caution said. "Can't stand them." He came over and gently held out his hand. "Name's Caution. You okay?"

"Christian," Christian said. "And yeah. I understand you caught me when I fainted."

"Knew you were gonna keel over," Caution said. "Just could tell. I was ready. That annoying guy in the booth is my little brother Boo-Boo. We're the Shepherd Brothers."

"Boo-Boo?" Christian said. Mike Hope smiled.

"It's a nickname," the speaker on the booth said.

"Boo-Boo and Caution Shepherd," Christian said. He was fully awake now, but felt like he was still asleep.

"You up to take a walk?" Caution asked.

"Uh…" Christian said and looked at his bare feet.

"We're just going to the roof," Caution said. "We'll get you some more coffee and another donut. Boo-Boo's got your stuff in the wash."

They walked down the ramp back to the office. Both Christian and Mike Hope took another donut. "You haven't eaten in a few days," Caution said. "You can take two or three."

Christian did. He balanced them on his NPR coffee mug and ate with the other hand. He and Hope followed the big man further down one more floor to an elevator. It was new and spotless and played a Muzak version of "Let It Be" as they rode the fifteen floors to the roof.

The stepped out into the morning sunshine and Caution tilted his head back to feel the breeze on his face. "I love it up here in the mornings."

Christian said, "Caution, why is there a parking garage this size in the middle of nowhere?"

"Everywhere is somewhere," Caution said. "No where is nowhere."

"Deep," Hope said.

"Thanks," Caution said. It was the only time Christian questioned anything about the garage.

Caution said, "I'm going to show you two things. One is not so nice and one is something wonderful, okay?"

Hope and Christian nodded. Caution walked them to the north end of the roof. He pointed. In the far distance Hope and Christian could see Denny Despair's giant purple gorilla waving in the breeze. Neither smiled. "Take a look at the gorilla," Caution said. "Now follow it to the left about a mile or so."

Both young men did. There was a dirt road that disappeared and reappeared in the trees, but eventually the road ended in what looked like a steep drop-off. At the bottom of the ravine were scattered bones and rags and skulls. Christian looked at Mike Hope as Hope started to weep. "You boys got lucky," Caution said. "Not everybody leaves Despair's place. Some spend their last days there."

He walked away and the travelers followed. Neither looked back. At the south end of the roof Caution pointed again, this time to a far distant light. At first Christian thought it was a reflection of the sun, but then saw that whatever it was, it was emitting its own light.

"It's the City of Light," Christian said.

Mike Hope smiled in relief.

"Not easy to get to," Caution said. "You've been through a lot and even though it looks close you're going to have to go through a lot to get there. My advice? Stay here another night, rest up, leave first thing. Build you strength up."

"But it's so close!" Christian said. He looked at Mike Hope. "We can leave as soon as our clothes are clean."

Hope looked at Caution. "You say we need to build up our strength. What you tink we have to do dat for? What we gonna find on our way?"

Caution looked at him but did not answer.

Hope looked at Christian. Christian said, "We're this close."

"Sup to you," Caution said.

Mike Hope sighed. "As soon as de clothes are ready and you tink of some way we can repay you for your kindness, we will be goin," Hope said quietly.

"No repayment," Caution said. "That's not how it works."

"Your stuff will be ready in an hour or so. Come, sit and rest. We'll talk about what you're going to need."

They followed Caution back to the elevator. Both Christian and Hope looked out at the City of Light in the distance. Both of them thinking, though not mentioning it to the other, that if they looked away it might disappear.

*****

Back in the office Boo-Boo was sitting behind the desk eating a donut and drinking coffee.

"They're going to move on," Caution said as he came into the room.

"Toldya they would, big brother."

Caution pulled two folding chairs from behind the door. He handed one to each of the young travelers and then sat down on the edge of the bed.

"Either of you two boys still have your scroll?"

"Scroll?" Christian asked.

"Your gizmo that the shiny guys gave you."

"Oh!" said Christian. "Yeah."

Mike Hope thought about the word "Scroll" and wondered exactly how long the Shepherd Brothers had been helping travelers.

Christian handed Caution his iPod. Caution flipped it over in his hand for a second, studying it.

"Gimmie that," Boo-boo said. He took it out of his brother's hand and plugged a small white cord into the bottom. He hit a button on his keyboard. "I'm downloading a map," he said. "You're going to come to a lot of forks in the road. You're going to need the map."

"Thanks," Christian said.

"I'm also giving you the new Green Day disc and some Miles Davis."

Caution scowled at his brother.

"What? It's a long walk."

Caution leaned in with his elbows on his knees. "I still think you should rest up and leave tomorrow, but since you're not going to do that, I can at least give you some advice."

Christian and Hope leaned in. "Stay away from butt-kissers," Caution said.

Christian and Hope nodded.

"And—this is it. There are no more rest stops. Once you start, this is the last leg of the journey. You don't stop until you get to the City of Light."

Christian smiled.

"No. I mean it!" Caution said. "Once you start you *don't stop*."

His earnestness almost made Christian and Hope rethink the whole leaving-right-away thing. Almost.

Chapter 17

With the parking garage and the Shepherd Brothers a mile or so behind them, Mike Hope was having trouble keeping up with Christian.

"Mon, you walkin' too fast. You gonna get careless."

"It's been so long," Christian said without looking behind him. "We're this close. I couldn't wait another day."

Hope walked faster to keep up with his energized friend. "Tomorrow we switch you to de-decaf," he said.

"Tomorrow," Christian said, "we'll wake up in the City of Light."

Mike Hope walked beside his friend now. They fell into a rhythm and were soon walking as one.

"We have time now," Christian said.

"Time for what?" Hope said.

"Time for your story. I told you mine. I never heard how you got on this path."

"Was the same Preacher man," Hope said.

"That's not enough," Christian said. "We've got miles to go. It's not even lunch and we'll be walking until it's night."

Hope was quiet for a few minutes and then said, "I was born on an island. My father own a little restaurant off de beaten path for tourists. My mother was de cook. My sister was de waitress. It was always expected of me that I go to work in de restaurant, meet a nice island girl and get married and take over the restaurant and den make more babies to do it all over again."

"And you didn't want to stay on the island all your life? Sounds kinda wonderful to me."

"Was kinda wonderful," Hope said. "Dat was de hard part. Was a really nice life and ev'eybody knew it was a nice life except dat I knew I was supposed to do something else."

"What?"

"I din know. I still don know. I know dat when I try to tell my family dat I don belong on the island de get all angry angry."

"When did you leave?"

"College," Hope said. "I lie to my parents. I tell dem I'm going to school so I can come back and run de bizness and dey can retire."

"You never went back, did you."

Hope shook his head. "I hurt my family very much. I go to school. I got no intention of going home so I don't go to class. I don't major in nothing' but drinking and trouble."

Christian didn't say anything.

"I spent all my time doing the party-party," Hope said. "De Jesus people with their perfect hair and their perfect faces and dere perfect names come knockin at my door telling me dat Jesus loves me and dat I be going to the fire place if I didn't stop with the party-party."

"How'd that go over?" Christian asked.

"Des perfect little people tell me I need to be like dem to be part of de Jesus family? Dey look boring to me. De look all clench up all de time. De smile, but it a smile like you see on de Barbie dolls. So Ken and Barbie tell me to change my ways I tell dem to go to hell. Two years I spend de nights drinking and feeling more and more empty-empty. I keep fillin the empty space with more drinking. I tought de only other way is to be with the Wonderbread people or de Atheist people, but dey look all angry-angry all de time. I wasn't angry-angry. I wasn't all happy-happy."

"What happened?"

"One weekend, it was a three-day weekend, which to me meant dat I could drink on Sunday too, I playin drinking games with a buncha guys in a dorm room and I don't remember the last part of it. I wake up layin' in a hallway of a building. In de basement. I got puke all over myself and I don't know how I got dere."

"Geez," Christian said.

"I find de door. I find I'm on de other side of town. I'm in somebody's apartment building but I don't know whose. I walk back to my dorm room and I go to take a shower and I find a note in my pocket."

He stopped walking. Christian did too. Hope said, "I never show dis to nobody." He pulled out his wallet. He rummaged past all the ticket stubs and receipts and finally came up with a card. He handed it to Christian.

It was a plain white business card. On the back was a handwritten note. It said, "When you get tired of waking up on the floor, call me."

The front of the card said, "Preacher," with a phone number.

"Ting was," Hope said, taking the card back, "he didn't help me. He didn't sit me up. He didn't try to save me. He didn't even give me an aspirin. Mon just see me laying dere in my own puke and put a note in my shirt. De happy-happy people, dey would have had a fundraiser and dragged me up in front of dere church and have a prayer meeting. Dis Preacher—he let me lay dere. I had to respect that. So de next day, I call.

"What happened?"

"I'm here walking with a white boy to the City of Light."

"I mean what else?" Christian said. "What did the Preacher say? Did you ever call your parents? Did you see the lady with the floppy hat? Did you see a cross?"

"De preacher, he give me a dope slap," Hope said, and laughed. "Den he gave me a book, but I lost it along dey way."

"Where?" Christian said,

"Back a ways. Bad place. I went off dey path and lose everything."

Christian knew what he meant. He thought of Faith again.

"That's where we met," Christian said.

"Met?" Mike Hope said. "Dat's de place where Hope come along and save your bacon."

"Did I thank you for that?"

"Many times," Hope said.

Soon the pair came to a fork in the road. They looked around but there were no signs. No engravings on the rocks. No arrows pointing one direction or another. They heard the motor before they saw the car. It was a very large motor.

Over the hill came a huge SUV. It was white. On the side door beneath a giant rearview mirror it said H-99.

It was the biggest car they had ever seen. The tires were white, the doors were white, the roof was white. A man in a white leather jacket and new white T-shirt leaned out as the vehicle slowed to a stop next to them.

"Where you boys headed?"

"The City of Light," Christian said.

"You two come all this way by yourselves? You must have the biggest stones I've ever heard of. Coming all this way on your own. That's truly cool."

Hope and Christian smiled a little.

"I never would have had the nerve to go by myself."

"Have you been there?" Christian asked.

"I live there," he said. "They sent me to get you."

"What?"

"They sent me to get you!" the driver said, cupping his hands over his mouth and shouting. He laughed. "Man, it is just so good to finally meet you. We keep track, you know, we watch people's journeys like we watch movies, and me—I been pullin for you guys for days now. You got this close and the boss says they walked enough, take the Hummer and go get them. So here I am."

Christian and Hope looked at him.

"Oh, where are my manners? My mother would have just boxed my ears! Forgive me, gentlemen." He got out of the Hummer and climbed down the short ladder and immediately climbed up the one next to the passenger door. He pulled it open and with a mock-bow said, "The chariot of the City of Light awaits you."

Christian and Mike Hope crawled up the ladder on the opposite side of the passenger door and slipped into the back seat.

The driver shut the door and crawled back down the ladder and up the one by the driver's door. He sat in the driver's seat and called back, "Buckle up now."

Without waiting he spun the Hummer around and was sailing down the road.

They bounced along on the comfortable seats. Christian was smiling ear to ear. He looked over at Mike Hope. His friend was not smiling at all. "What's wrong?"

Mike Hope frowned and leaned forward. He pressed his finger against the white leather seatback in front of him. He pulled his hand away and showed Christian the white paint on his finger. Christian reached into his bag and pulled out one of the spare T-shirts the Shepherd Brothers had given him. He wiped the seatback, taking away a large section of white paint. Beneath it was a black of absolute ebony. Mike Hope turned around and saw they were traveling in the exact wrong direction.

"Dis is not going to be good," he said.

The driver looked at him in the mirror. "You made that easy," he said, and sped up.

The driver focused his attention on Christian and Hope and did not see what was ahead of him in the road. He turned back around in time to see the figure in the shiny white armor. Full armor. Head to toe. Spear. Shield. Sword. The whole bit. Standing there in the road ten feet tall or more. The SUV did not have time to stop or swerve.

The driver screamed. Christian and Hope screamed.

The H-99 hit the Angel in the road at 85 miles an hour with the same result as if it had hit a ten-foot-tall three-feet-in-circumference steel pole.

Christian and Mike Hope sailed forward and through the glass of the front windshield. The Angel held out her arms like a cross and each young man sailed into an arm. Hard. They hit the angel's arms and fell backward onto the dirt. The SUV crumpled like a paper airplane folding in on itself. In one brief moment, all four tires were off the ground. The SUV slammed back onto the road about one-third the size it had been a moment ago.

The Angel looked down at Christian and Hope. Both were lying on their backs. Both were gasping for the air that had been forced out of their lungs when they "hit" the Angel.

The Angel, (who was now only about eight feet tall and wearing a white robe with the traditional fluffy wings) grabbed each of the young travelers by the collar and dragged them to the side of the road. She stood there waiting for them to catch their breath. Reaching down, she grabbed each one by the shirtfront and stood them on their feet.

"What was the last thing the Shepherds told you to watch out for?" she scolded.

"Butt-kissers," Christian said, still trying to catch his breath.

"And when you came to the fork in the road, why didn't you use the map that the Shepherds gave you?"

"We forgot," Mike Hope said.

"What did we learn?" the Angel asked as she folded her arms and scowled.

"Angels are hard," Mike Hope said, holding his stomach.

"We learned to listen and do what we're told or we'll never see the City of Light," Christian said.

"Butt-kisser," Hope said.

Christian looked up, but the Angel had gone. The Hummer H-99 sat on its nose in the middle of the road. It was folded like an accordion. The rear wheels were still spinning. There was no movement from inside—which could have had something to do with the fact that the rear bumper was only about four feet from the front bumper.

Chapter 18

Christian and Mike Hope continued along the path. Christian occasionally rubbed his chest where he had collided with the Angel.

"In all de Sunday school books we have at de church weh I grow up," Mike Hope said, "All de angels are soft and fluffy. Dey carry babies and fly around. Dat one was very solid." He gingerly touched his own chest as if he were searching for a bruise.

It was then that Christian and Mike Hope saw something they thought they'd never see. With all the things they'd seen since leaving their respective cities and setting out on this journey, they saw what they thought was nearly impossible. They saw someone coming the other way.

He was a tall man, and he wore a suit and tie. The coat was draped over one arm and he had unbuttoned the collar of his white shirt, which remained crisp and clean. There was no sign of fatigue on him. He saw them too and smiled. It was a smile that seemed insincere at best. At worst it seemed like someone who had just eaten a small child.

"Politician?" Hope whispered.

"I was thinking insurance," Christian replied.

"Gentlemen," the approaching man said. He held out a clean hand and both the weary and disheveled travelers shook it. "Fine day, isn't it?"

Christian and Hope nodded. They had become wary of other travelers and were waiting to see what happened next.

"Headed for the City of Light, are you?" the man said. His tone had become condescending. His smile changed as well. When Christian had been in a junior high youth group and the youth pastor would ask a question which Christian thought required opinion and the pastor thought required scripture quotation, the youth pastor would smile in the same way that this man did. Christian had a word for it. The word Christian thought of was "snarky."

"We are going to the City of Light," Hope said. He kept his answer simple. There was something about this guy that made him uneasy.

"Let me save you the time," the man said. "It's not there."

Christian and Hope looked at each other. Christian said, "What do you mean it's not there?"

"I mean it isn't there." He chuckled.

Christian looked at Hope. "We took the wrong path again?"

"Not the wrong path," the man said. "I mean it doesn't exist. There is no such place. It would appear that you gentlemen have traveled a long way." He stepped back and looked them up and down. "A *very* long way—for no reason whatsoever."

"It has to be there!" Christian said.

"I've just come from that direction," the man said shaking his head, "and I can tell you, there's nothing there. You should go back the way you came."

Hope looked at the man calmly. "De City of Light has always been dere and always will be dere."

The man glanced over at Mike Hope as if he was just now noticing the dreads. "You've come a *very very* long way, haven't you, my friend? That just shows how far the lie travels."

"What are you talking about?" Christian said. His voice cracked just slightly. When it did the man in the suit turned on him.

"I mean it's all a lie. It's a lie that has been perpetuated for generations. There's no God. No Jesus. No divine breath moving about. It's a story that was made up by people in power to make people who don't have power behave."

Christian looked at Hope, but Hope was still staring at the man in the suit.

"Oh come on!" the man said. "Don't tell me you've never questioned the whole goofy story."

They were silent.

"Not even once?" He was openly laughing at them now. He unfolded his suit coat from his arm and fished in the inside pocket. "Gentlemen, I work with a firm called Awareness Thinking Establishes Individual Standard Thinking."

He handed each of them a business card that said simply, A.Th.E.I.S.T. At the bottom of the card was his name: Judge Alan Doubt.

"You're a judge?" Christian asked.

"Retired," the man said.

"You don't look old enough to be retired," Mike Hope said.

"Took an early retirement when that whole Ten Commandments bugaboo started."

"Let me guess," Mike Hope said. "You weren't in favor of de commandments being in de courthouse."

"That's when I started the firm," Doubt said. "We represent clients that have perfectly common sense problems and cases that can't get past a system that insists on using the existence of a supreme being as its basis for justice."

"And you came all dis way to…." Hope left the sentence open.

"Prove the point," Doubt said. "See, it's all about proof. That's what our legal system is based on. Proof. If you can smell it, touch it, taste it, see it, hear it…then it exists. You can't do any of that with this so-called 'God,' so it has no business as a factor in our decision-making."

When Judge Alan Doubt said the word "God" he made air quotes and rolled his eyes. It was then that Christian was ready to keep moving. Mike Hope was not.

"You came all dis way and you din see de City of Light and dat's proof enough for you dat God does not exist."

"I'm telling you it isn't there. It never was," Doubt said.

"So you created an organization to tell us dat?" Hope said.

"What do you mean?" the Judge said.

Mike Hope said, "We saw a giant inflatable purple gorilla in a green dress. We know der is no such ting in dis life as a real giant purple gorilla in a green dress yet we don't have no organization to tell us dat. Why do we need you to tell us der is no God?"

"I represent people who have been taken advantage of because of the lie," the Judge said flatly.

"We've seen so much," Christian offered. "We've experienced it."

"Trick of the mind," Doubt said. "You go through something horrific and you think that God is punishing you. You go through something wonderful and you think that God is rewarding you. It's coincidence, my friend. That's all. You assign this coincidence to a deity because you've been taught to do so by other people who also can't take responsibility for their own actions."

"God exists," Christian said. He wanted to make it sound final, but despite all he had been through, a trace of fear crept into his voice.

"Can you prove it?" the Judge said. "Can you offer me evidence? *Any* evidence? Do you have anything on you right now that would show me one single tiny piece of empirical evidence that this supreme being exists?

"It's about Faith," Christian said. He was thinking of his friend he had been waiting to see again. He thought about her image on the coffee cup and how incredibly stressed he had been when he saw it and how it had simply changed to a Tom Hanks quote.

"Faith is a cop out," Judge Doubt said. "It just means you can't prove your point, so you go hide behind the word faith. You can't offer me one single solitary bit of proof that all our actions aren't in vain. But if it's this magical belief in an all-seeing all-knowing being that trips your trigger, then by all means, go for it."

Judge Alan Doubt reached out and attempted to put his hand on Mike Hope's shoulder. Hope batted it away as if it had a booger on it.

"Don't get testy with me," Doubt said, "just because you can't prove your point, just because you're afraid to look like a fool after all this time."

Hope stared at him.

Judge Doubt took a step in front of Mike Hope and narrowed his eyes. "How can you do it? How can you look at this messed-up world and still believe that there is a God of unconditional love up there watching us all?"

"I decided to," Mike Hope said.

"What?" Doubt asked.

"I decided to," Hope repeated. He took a deep breath and calmed himself. Mentally stepping out of the confrontation, he said, "You and I are on an equal playing field."

"Not really," Doubt said. "You see I have…"

"Pretty much the same information as the rest of us," Mike finished for him. "You and me and everybody else all have the same information available to us. We can study and search and talk and listen to people all over de world and we come up with de same answers. But me? I decided to believe."

Doubt scowled.

"I decide to be a believer and to live my life dat way. I have spent my life supporting my decision wit my life. Everyday, I live like I believe I am loved by sometin' bigger dan myself. You, you took de same information and you decide not to believe. You spend your life supporting dat decision wit de way you live. So basically, you and I, we starting at de same place right now. I have faith. You don't."

The man turned toward Christian. Christian thought for a moment that the man looked shorter than he had a minute ago. Doubt opened his mouth to speak, but Christian interrupted him. "Tell me about the God you don't believe in."

"What?" the Judge said.

"Tell me about the God you don't believe in," Christian said again. Mike Hope's speech had strengthened him.

"I don't know what you mean," Judge Doubt said.

"Yes, you do," Hope offered.

"This God you say does not exist," Christian said. "Tell me about God."

The Judge smirked. "An invisible being who lives far away and watches everyone and puts these incredible expectations on people....who judges who is and who isn't good enough for His almighty attention. This is a God who will send you to a place of everlasting torment and damnation if you break any one of his rules, who gave you a brain to use and then apparently condemns you when you actually use it. He wants to be put first and then punishes you when you do not. Who apparently can fix everything, all problems, but chooses not to. Who allows children to die of starvation, wars to be fought over stupid ideas, and unspeakable evil to exist, and then has the gall to say, 'I love you.' Is that what you mean?"

Christian said, "Funny, I don't believe in that God either." Christian walked around the Judge and started down the road again. Mike Hope followed him.

Hope whispered, "Now *dat* was an exit line."

Christian smiled. "No. This is…" He turned back to the judge and said, "Judge?"

The Judge turned and looked at him.

"Do you want to come with us?"

The Judge put on his coat and turned away. "You've been deceived," he called after them.

"What a coincidence!" Hope called. "So have you!"

As they walked over the hill, Christian said, "'So have you'? I finally get a great exit line and you have to go and throw another one in?"

"Sorry," Mike Hope said. "Seemed funny when I thought of it."

Chapter 19

They continued to walk. As they crested the next hill they saw a park bench and a lamppost. Beneath the post, sitting on a bench, was a frazzled-looking man in a wrinkled suit. He had a huge stack of files in his lap and seemed to be frantically searching for something in one of them.

"Sir?" Christian spoke and the man jumped nervously.

"What?" he said. "I have it here. Just a second."

"Cut back on de caffeine, mon," Hope said.

"Huh?" the nervous man asked. He began flipping through the papers as fast as he could. "I'm sorry. I know it's here if you'll just give me a moment."

"What are you looking for?" Christian asked.

"My baptismal certificate," the man said. "I'll have it for you in just a moment."

"Why do you think we need your baptismal certificate?"

The man looked up and ran a hand through his already disheveled hair. "You're not from the City of Light?"

"We're just on our way," Christian said. "We're not there yet."

"Oh thank heavens!" the man said. "I thought you were with the shining ones." He held out is hand. "Igor."

"Igor?" Hope asked.

"My mother liked old horror movies," Igor said. "My name is Igor Nance."

"I am Hope," Mike Hope said. He held out his hand. "This is Christian."

Igor Nance shook them both. "Oh, such wonderful names! How am I going to get through the gate with a name like Igor?"

"I don't think they'll mind," Christian said. He was trying to be reassuring.

"I've never been good with paperwork," Nance said, "and I know I'm not getting in on my good looks."

"Did you mean the angels?" Christian asked. "Before, when you said 'the shining ones.' Did you mean the angels?"

"Aren't we supposed to call them the shining ones?" the man asked.

"Angels is what my mother called them," Mike Hope said. "I din know der was a proper word."

"You have to use the proper words or they won't let you in," Nance said. He looked up at them in a puzzle and said, "You don't have your paperwork."

"We have de Bible," Hope said.

"Did you memorize it?" Nance said.

"We've read it," Christian said. "Well, most of it."

"Oh, you're in trouble!" Igor Nance said. "You're not getting in."

"I don't understand," Christian said.

Nance was now visibly upset by the situation. "You have to have the right paperwork or a least a letter explaining your circumstances. It's all points. Look..."

He opened the file that was on the top of the stack on his lap and showed them a collection of coloring book pages that looked as though they had been colored by a three-year-old.

"See?" he said. "That was my work. Now look how much better I did later." He held out another picture. This one was of Joseph and his coat of many colors. "See how I stayed in the lines?"

"Impressive," Mike Hope said and looked at Christian for some sort of non-verbal confirmation that this guy was off his nut.

"I have my Sunday school certificates from grades K-12. I have my confirmation certificate. And I have a collection of all the pictures I ever took on the high school mission trips." He waved a flash-drive in the air. It looked like Jesus carrying a lamb. "You don't think they'll want real photos, do you? Do you think they'll accept them on this?"

"I'm sure they're pretty up to date," Christian said. He looked at Mike Hope and made a face.

"Who told you that you needed all this stuff?" Mike Hope asked.

"Everybody says so," Igor said. "Everybody has to have the right forms. The credits you have determine how big your heavenly palace is."

"You get your own palace?" Christian asked.

"Some of us do," Igor said. "Others get to spend eternity in a shack."

"I don't understand," Christian said.

"How did you get this far?"

"It's been a long strange trip," Hope put in.

"Well, all I know is that some people get a palace of gold and others get a little shack and others don't get in at all."

"Sounds like earth," Hope said.

"Oh, this is much better," Nance said. He folded an envelope and slid it into a file by itself.

Christian sat down on the bench and said, "What if you don't need them? What if you can just walk in?"

"You can't just walk in!" Nance said. "You have to earn it."

"How long have you been sitting here?"

"I've forgotten," Nance said.

"Which way did you come from?"

"I don't remember. Ah! Here it is." Nance pulled out a small beige card with a gold sticker on the front. He ran his fingers along the printed card as if he had just found the holy grail. "Now I can get in."

He began to search for the proper file in which to put the card.

"But what if..." Mike Hope said, "what if you were born in another place and had no idea about de father and de son and de holy-holy. What if you din get de baptizing?"

Igor Nance looked up at him with pity in his eyes. "Oh, I am soooo sorry. You've come such a long way. Look, nobody knows what's going to happen once you get to the gate. Maybe they'll let you take a test or something."

"What about grace?" Christian asked.

"What about it?" Nance argued. He was lightly tapping the papers on the top of his file stack to even them up."

"I mean what's the purpose of grace if you still have to prove you can get in with the right forms?"

"Some people don't deserve grace," Nance said. For just a moment it was as if Christian and Hope could see him thinking of someone in specific.

"Dat's why it's grace," Hope said. "Grace is when you are given what you don't deserve."

"Not everyone," Nance said. "Look, I spent my whole life putting these files together. You think I would have done all this if you could just walk in? Nobody walks in. You have to get down on your knees and ask forgiveness. You have to renounce your sin. You have to pray the sinner's prayer." He looked up at them. "Oh, tell me you at least know the sinner's prayer."

"Din know dey had der own prayer," Hope said.

"Oh my," Nance said. The look of pity had returned. "I do hope that He's in a good mood."

"Who?"

"The Gatekeeper," Nance said. He sighed and said, "Did you ever go to Sunday school?"

"Never paid attention much," Christian said.

"The Gatekeeper checks his book and sees how good you were."

"Like Santa," Hope said.

Igor Nance glared at him. "You're this close and you're going to crack jokes?"

"Dey don like jokes?"

"Maybe inside," Igor said, "but the gate is serious business. My mother used to tell me when I was little that you had to stand before the big gate and they checked your name in the big book and if you were bad they pushed a button and a trap door opened and you fell down into hell."

"That's a horrible thing to teach a child," Christian said.

"It made me behave," Nance said, "made me be a good boy. I'm glad she did it. No telling how I might have turned out."

"Seems like der be a whole lot of people on earth who wouldn't know about de paperwork rule," Hope said. "Not everybody is a Jesus follower."

"Not everybody gets in," Nance said. "Some people aren't going to get even close." Christian could tell he wanted to say something more but didn't. Igor Nance slid his hand into the pocket of his suit jacket. "Uh-oh."

"What's uh-oh?" Christian asked.

Nance said, "I had extra credit and now I can't find it?"

"Extra credit?"

"Once they see all my good works I was going to pull out this picture I had of me and Billy Graham."

"You had your picture taken with Billy Graham so that you could get extra credit when you got to the City of Light?" Hope asked. He said it aloud as though he was repeating it for his own ears.

"Could be the difference between silver and gold bricks," Nance said. "Might get me a better neighborhood."

"There's some sort of heavenly zoning committee?" Christian asked, amazed.

"Well, yes," Nance said. He was starting to flip through the files again.

"So de streets of gold dey turn into streets of aluminum foil in certain parts of heaven?" Mike Hope asked.

"Again with the jokes?"

Christian stood up. "Do you want to walk with us?"

"No No," Nance said. "I need to find my picture and I'd prefer to go in on my own." He looked up at the two of them. His meaning seemed clear. He didn't want the two of them affecting his entrance.

Christian looked at Mike Hope and they both started off down the path again. Mike Hope turned back. "Do you want help?"

"No...I've got this...really," Nance said. He was checking his pockets again.

Christian and Hope started up the path. They walked just about another mile when they heard the hum.

"Do you feel that?" Christian asked.

"What?"

"When you were a kid did you ever lay your head on a railroad track to see if you could hear the train coming?"

"Din have a lot of trains on my island," Mike said.

Christian squatted down and put his hand flat on the ground. "Feel this."

Hope bent down on one knee and put his hand down too. "Good vibrations," he said, and smiled.

"We're close," Christian said. He started to run up the hill. Mike Hope followed him.

They reached the top of the hill and saw the City of Light.

In front of it

between it and them

was a River

a very large, very angry, very deep-looking River.

There was no bridge.

Chapter 20

With the sun setting behind them both Christian and Hope had to shield their eyes from the glow that exploded from the City of Light.

It was unlike anything either of them had ever seen. There were buildings that seemed to have been designed without taking the laws of physics into account, and yet they stood. There were colors so bright that both Christian and Hope suspected that the City itself was simply containing the colors inside its borders, that once they passed through the gates the colors would continue on either side of the rainbow.

There was a deep sense that music was playing, but that it was muffled—not by the walls of the city, but by a lack of awareness on how to hear it. Neither moved for a full minute. Christian started down the hill toward the raging River.

The sound of the water drowned out any sense of music coming from the city. There was an Angel waiting for them by the bank. It was the same Angel who had caught them when they were thrown through the window of the giant hummer. She was still tall, but her expression had softened. The feathers in her wings blew gently in the breeze caused by the River behind her.

"My travelers. My pilgrims," she said quietly when they stood before her. She put out her hand and gently touched Christian's cheek with the back of her fingers. Christian felt a warmth surge through him, like the opening chord of an orchestra tuning his soul.

The Angel brushed Mike Hope's dreads back and he closed his eyes. Christian knew he felt the same feeling surge through him.

"So long a journey," she said. "So many things learned."

She touched Christian again and her eyebrows furrowed slightly, but her smile did not falter. "Still so many questions. Why so many questions, my pilgrim?"

"My family," Christian said, "Faith. The people in the City of Ruin. I just need to know…"

"Shhhhhhhhhhhhhhhh," she said, and placed a finger on his lips. Christian smelled the Angel's hand. It smelled like peppermint lifesavers, wedding cake frosting, and clean sheets on a clothesline. "Just have faith."

She looked at Mike Hope's eyes. "You are loved. Don't ever forget that."

They both nodded.

"You have one more thing to do before you enter the City."

Both Hope and Christian looked past her to the River. The sun was setting behind the hill and the water seemed to grow darker.

"The River…" she said, "the River is deep, but its depth is linked to your faith. The River is wild, but its force is linked to your soul."

Christian said, "I don't understand."

The Angel smiled. It was an understanding smile. "How deep your faith is," she said, "is how shallow the River is. How raging the waters are…is how strong your soul needs to be to cross."

Still slightly unsure, the two pilgrims moved forward. They could feel the mist of the water against their faces. They stood there next to each other and then hugged like brothers.

Simultaneously they stepped into the swell. The water seemed to rush at their feet, but to the two travelers it seemed like they had stepped into a child's wading pool.

Two steps and then three. They looked at each other, but they did not look back.

Four steps.

On the fifth step Christian suddenly felt like he had stepped off the edge of an underwater shelf and was immediately engulfed by the water. He sunk below the surface. Mike Hope, who had been standing just a step downriver "felt" Christian pass beneath him. He turned back and looked at the Angel. She seemed neither concerned nor joyful. "The River is never the same for everyone," she said.

Ten feet downriver Christian's head burst through the surface and he gasped for air. Hope jumped to his left and found himself up to his waist in the same spot where Christian was up to his neck. There was a rock and Christian grabbed it and hung on. The water's rage grew and blasted against them.

"You go," Christian said.

Mike Hope grabbed his hand and yanked him from the rock. He took only a few steps and looked back. He was clutching Christian's hand and saw that the water that rushed over his friend was turning gray. A long stream of guilt and hate and anxiety and worry and stress flowed out of Christian's skin as the water flowed angrily over them. Mike Hope stumbled and fell. He thought he was going to sink beneath the surface himself, but he did not.

"Leave me," Christian yelled above the din.

"Stand up, mon!" he screamed. "Find your footing."

Mike Hope was sure the ground beneath his own feet at the bottom of the River had turned to sand. He felt his feet sink in and for a moment he could push on no further.

"I am stuck," Hope shouted.

Christian's head disappeared beneath the surface and Mike Hope felt two hands on his trapped foot. When it was free he moved forward, but had no idea what happened to Christian. He turned around and saw no one.

"Here!" Christian shouted. Hope turned and saw Christian, now fifteen feet in front of him, standing on the surface of the water and smiling. Hope thought his own feet were made of rock.

"I cannot move."

"Leave it!" Christian shouted at him. "Leave it on the bottom."

Mike Hope took a deep breath and felt his pain drop out of him. His guilt at leaving his family. His shame at the way he had once lived. He felt these fall out of him and sink beneath the soil under his feet. He felt lighter. He felt lighter than he had in years. The River had taken from him what he had never been able to leave behind on his own. His next step brought him higher in the River. He shoved himself forward, nearly stumbling as the last piece of darkness in his soul sank beneath him. He stood on the water's surface. He reached out to Christian, who grabbed his hand and pulled his friend closer. Soaking wet, they embraced again, this time laughing.

They took two more steps before collapsing on the riverbank. They could both feel the ground vibrating under their backs. They looked up to see the Angel looking down on them and smiling.

"That wasn't so bad, was it?" she asked.

Christian and Mike Hope both began to laugh. They stood, feeling as if they had just slept for three days.

Their energy seemed boundless, their bodies light. They hugged once more and saw that the Angel was now at the top of the hill in front of them. They ran after her. Getting near the top, they saw a wall. Higher than they could see. In the path in front of them, a door, fifty feet high and every inch carved with ornate pictures of their own struggle. Christian put his hand on the door. The vibration had a rhythm now. A drum beat. The Angel grabbed hold of the handle with both hands and pulled. When the door had opened just enough for a human body to fit through—

Faith burst through from the other side and into Christian's arms. She hugged him and kissed the top of his head seven times. He held her close to him and began to weep.

"The band," she shouted! "You won't believe the band!"

Christian said, "Faith, this is Hope."

She turned and threw herself into Hope's arms too. "I love your name," Faith said.

Hope smiled.

She grabbed each of them by the hand and yanked them through the gate into the City of Light.

9 781940 671475